'Why did you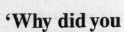

A cynical spark l
spoke. 'Because y
invitation if I had told you the truth.'

'Tell me, then, Alexos, exactly what employment are you offering me?'

'My key to entering Belvedere once more is to prove myself a reformed character. What better proof than to bring with me my future wife?'

Dear Reader

For many of us, this is the best period of the year—the season of goodwill and celebration—though it can make big demands on your time and pocket, too! Or, maybe you prefer to spend these mid-winter months more quietly? Whatever you've got planned, Mills & Boon's romances are always there for you as special friends at the turn of the year: easy, entertaining and comforting reads that are great value for money. Stay warm, won't you!

The Editor

Angela Wells was educated in an Essex convent, and later left the bustling world of media marketing and advertising to marry and start a family in a suburb of London. Writing started out as a hobby, and she used backgrounds she knows well from her many travels, especially in the Mediterranean area. Her ambition, she says, in addition to writing many more romances, is to spend more time in Australia—especially Sydney and the islands of the Great Barrier Reef.

RECKLESS DECEPTION

BY

ANGELA WELLS

MILLS & BOON LIMITED
ETON HOUSE   18-24 PARADISE ROAD
RICHMOND   SURREY   TW9 1SR

*First published in Great Britain 1992
by Mills & Boon Limited*

© Angela Wells 1992

*Australian copyright 1992
Philippine copyright 1993
This edition 1993*

ISBN 0 263 77861 4

*Set in Times Roman 10 on 12 pt.
01-9301-55543 C*

Made and printed in Great Britain

CHAPTER ONE

'I HOPE you will understand and be happy for me!' That was what Philip had written.

Ilona stared down into the depths of the tall glass she held in her hand before taking a reflective sip. The potent El Greco special was quite a change from her usual iced coffee. A rueful smile curled the corners of her pretty full-lipped mouth as she recalled Manolis's quick look of surprise as he'd made it for her. Thankfully it was her free evening—no courier duties lined up for her to-night—and she'd really felt the need for something to anaesthetise the pain after receiving that totally unex-pected letter from the man who twelve months ago had asked her to marry him. Unfortunately the remedy didn't appear to be working.

At least, she tried to comfort herself, she had the prospect of a further three months working for Happy Hellenic Holidays on Crete—an island which had already fulfilled all her expectations of it. Taking another sip from the cocktail, she coughed as it stung her throat, before settling back in her chair and casually observing the bar, which was beginning to get crowded as guests came in for an after-dinner drink.

Her large dark brown eyes moved thoughtfully to-wards Manolis, noting compassionately how deathly pale he looked and how one side of his pleasant face was puffy and swollen.

Of course, he should have gone to the dentist several days ago when he had first experienced an aching tooth;

instead he'd struggled on, hoping the matter would resolve itself. Clearly it hadn't. From the fine film of perspiration she could see on his brow, she realised he was in considerable pain. Hopefully, for his sake, it would be a quiet night.

Glancing behind her as a burst of laughter announced the arrival of a party of young Swedes, she turned again sharply as she heard Manolis's voice raised suddenly and unexpectedly.

'I'm sorry, *kyrie*, but we don't serve Greeks at this hotel.'

'*Oriste*?' The word sliced through the air with the resonance that only a Greek could perfect, its inflexion expressing a range of emotions from sheer disbelief to puzzlement and on to the extremity of anger. As she was instantly aware of the latent atmosphere of aggression that hovered between the two men, Ilona's heartbeat quickened in sympathy with Manolis's reaction.

'It's a rule of the management,' he said abruptly. 'We only serve tourists.'

'Do you, now?'

Her eyes swept over the speaker, her ears registering the deep timbre of the lazy reply. Inoffensive in themselves, the words promised an intractability that threatened trouble. Normally Manolis would be well able to deal with the matter, but this evening, suffering as he was, she knew it was a hassle he could well do without.

Watching as the newcomer rested one lean hip on a bar stool while the other foot remained stolidly on the floor, she estimated his height. Well over six feet tall, she decided. In fact, the impact of his physical presence was quite startling. Continuing to regard him covertly, she found herself intrigued by the hard, uncompromising bones of his nose and jaw, and the curve and sweetness of a short upper lip balanced by a generous, sensual lower one, the whole contentious face crowned by blue-black hair, thick and springy, framing the broad sweep of his forehead, clinging in tendrils on the nape of his neck.

It wasn't only his face and build that made him such an imposing adversary either. Even from where she was sitting, she could sense a powerful personality, an arrogance of manner, which had to be based on something more substantial than the mere juxtaposition of bone and flesh and muscle!

A man of dangerous potential, she judged, unable to control the consequent shiver that trembled down her spine. Somewhere in his early thirties, this was no juvenile who would slink away humiliated by his rebuttal: neither was he a typical middle-aged merchant who would be embarrassed at the hotel's bigotry and be only too eager to escape from the situation. No, she decided, quelling a small spasm of apprehension, this man undoubtedly spelt trouble.

As if to reinforce her opinion, he leant forward slightly, fixing Manolis with a deep stare.

'You may refuse to serve me if my clothes or manner offend you, and I will leave without argument . . .' there was a tightly held fury in his deep voice now '. . . but the hell I'll go before I'm ready—just because I'm Greek!' As he spoke he rose to face the barman square on, his hand gripping the rail against the bar with such force that the knuckles showed white.

Surely some other member of staff would see what was happening and go to Manolis's aid? The last thing the barman needed in his present state of health was a punch-up! She cast a desperate glance round the crowded room. No one. Her despair deepened. That meant it was up to her to defuse the situation if trouble was to be averted. It was the least she could do for the man who had offered her the hospitality of his home from time to time since her arrival in Crete three months previously.

With a small sigh that acknowledged the inevitability of her action, she rose to her feet and approached the two men, her high heels clicking an accompaniment to her determined progress.

'I'm sorry to interrupt...' she began a trifle breathlessly as she reached the scene of incipient combat, her heart beating a rapid tattoo in response to her own interference. Instantly she became the focus of two pairs of male eyes. Swallowing nervously, she prayed for inspiration and found it. 'But I think this gentleman has come to keep an appointment with me.' She smiled winningly at Manolis, who was regarding her expressionlessly. 'I'm sorry, Manolis, I should have warned you I was expecting a visitor to discuss the possibility of including boat trips in our special holiday attractions for our clients at this hotel!'

'Boat trips?'

Aware of the growing disbelief on Manolis's distorted face, and not daring to look at the stranger, who stood silently beside her, she battled on, determined to save Manolis from further altercation whether he appreciated it or not. The management of the hotel was incredibly strait-laced, and if it came to a brawl Manolis might very well lose his job, even though the fracas was not of his making.

'Of course, I should have remembered to wear my uniform,' she continued brightly, forcing a laugh from nervous lips as she glanced down at the pretty mint and lilac crêpe de Chine dress with its short sleeves and softly gathered skirt, which she had chosen from her limited personal wardrobe. 'I was sitting over there so deep in thought that I'm afraid I didn't notice you arrive.' Fighting down her growing feeling of unease as Manolis looked more disapproving than grateful, she turned for the first time to confront the tall Greek at her side. 'I'm Ilona Frankard of Happy Hellenic Holidays,' she explained sweetly. 'It was me you were looking for, wasn't it?'

Unprepared for the full impact of his attention as he regarded her with cynical deliberation from between thick, spiky eyelashes with eyes of such a dark blue that they were almost violet, she felt a warm wave of blood pinken her cheeks, and silently cursed herself for the embarrassing tendency she had to blush at the slightest provocation.

Surely this awkward stranger was bright enough to realise she was offering him peace with honour? Yet the expression on his face showed no sign of gratitude. Only when she saw his clenched fist unfurl, his stiff shoulders flex beneath the close-fitting pale blue shirt which graced them and the pugnacious jawline slacken a little did she feel able to exhale a breath of relief.

'Ilona Frankard.' He repeated her name with a deeply mocking awareness, his sensuous mouth fulfilling its inherent promise by parting to show perfect teeth. 'Yes, indeed. I didn't realise it when I walked in here, but you are exactly what I was looking for!'

His voice was cultured and polite but there was a gleam in his indigo eyes that unnerved her. She had spoken in Greek but he had guessed her nationality and chosen English for his reply. Had his error in selecting a pronoun been intentional? Well, she comforted herself, it appeared she'd managed to avert a crisis anyway. All that remained now was to see that this troublemaker got his drink, then, male pride vindicated—he could get lost!

Mustering all her dignity, she ordered herself another 'special' from Manolis before turning her raised eyebrows in the direction of her unwelcome guest.

'As I said, I'll have an ouzo, ice, and light on the water.' He accepted her invitation with a slight bow, placing a firm hand beneath her elbow. 'Over there.' He nodded to indicate an empty table for two at the far end of the bar, allowing her just enough time to see Manolis dip his head in curt acceptance of the order, before leading her firmly away from the bar.

'Was that really necessary?' Facing him across the small table, she raised her smooth brows, the contempt in her voice matching her steady appraisal of his dark countenance.

'Insisting on being served in a public hotel?' An unrecognised emotion flickered in his clear eyes, and she was conscious of their lazy regard of her face, framed by the smooth bell of honey-gold hair. 'I consider it was. I detest racism in any form.'

'So do I,' she affirmed instantly. 'But in this case Manolis was only doing his job.' Shifting uneasily in her chair, she was too aware of the brilliance of his penetrating regard to be at ease. 'That's not to say I agree with the policy, and naturally I understand why you...why all the other Greeks around here resent the situation. It was brought in to prevent the bar becoming crowded with groups of young Greek men looking for...' She hesitated, embarrassed by his obvious amusement.

'Looking for what most young Greek men want!' He finished her sentence blandly. 'The same thing, incidentally, which most young northern European ladies are only too eager to provide, *ne*?'

Ilona shrugged. There was no way she intended becoming involved in a discussion on morals with this irritating upstart, although privately she admitted that some of her younger female clients showed little discrimination in the holiday liaisons they formed, either in quality or number!

'It's only been open for three months, and the management are particularly anxious to develop it to appeal to an up-market clientele and are marketing its attributes through carefully selected travel agents,' she informed him coolly. 'As it's the first large hotel on this stretch of coast, it does attract a great deal of attention, and they feel that if the bar becomes packed with the cream of young Greek manhood, seeking to add new meaning to pan-European co-operation, many of the older, wealthier clients will be discouraged from spending their money in the bar and seek their evening entertainment elsewhere. So, rather than discriminate between individual Greeks, they decided to ban Greek nationals altogether.'

Dark eyebrows rose sardonically. 'Not only a decision of doubtful legality, I would have thought,' the stranger returned evenly, 'but also of doubtful logic.' The dark blue eyes swept comprehensively around the room. 'In my opinion there are several ladies present who would welcome the presence of the cream of young Greek manhood with open arms at the very least.'

Determined not to be diverted by the fact that privately she shared his opinion, Ilona frowned. 'The point is,' she declared primly, 'that Manolis isn't personally responsible for the decision and you had no cause to brawl with him! Particularly as anyone with half an eye could see that he's far from well, and probably unable to defend himself adequately against assault at the moment.'

'Assault!' Anger, cold and piercing, stung her across the table. Automatically Ilona recoiled as the lean body opposite bent towards her. 'Why should you suppose I intended to assault him?'

Eyes bleak and dark as a winter sky demanded an answer as a large hand moved with purposeful speed to imprison her smaller fist as it lay half tensed on the table.

Astonished that her rebuke had summoned forth so strong a reaction, she raised a defiant chin, too conscious of the roughness of his palm against her skin to be at ease as she met his narrowed gaze with assumed confidence.

'It was your body language,' she retorted spiritedly. 'Your fists were clenched and all your muscles were tensed up. It was only a matter of time before you lashed out...'

As he said nothing, but continued to stare at her with cold contempt, she became increasingly regretful of the reckless decision which had landed her with such an abrasive companion. It wasn't as if she was certain that Manolis had appreciated her effort either! She was sure the Greek barman had seen right through her subterfuge and was none too pleased with her action, despite her good intentions. If only he would hurry up with their order, enabling her to escape from the trap she had made for herself!

Her discomfort growing beneath the steely regard of her companion, she sighed. Enough of tilting at windmills, she lectured herself silently. It wouldn't be the first time her ready sympathy had landed her in trouble, but in this instance discretion was probably the better part of valour.

'Well, all right, then...if you deny it, perhaps I was mistaken; but that's the impression I got.' She regarded his aggressive countenance with calm dislike.

'You were mistaken.' His voice was marginally less icy as his grasp on her hand relaxed. 'It seems you are not such an expert on body language as you would like to think. I don't deny I was angry, but I had no intention of striking your boyfriend.'

'Manolis isn't my boyfriend.' As she was angered by the condescension of his tone, her retort was more heated than perhaps the remark justified, but it was too late to retract it. 'He happens to be a married man with four daughters.'

'Splendid! Then I have no need to fear his jealousy.' For the first time since they'd reached the table her unwelcome companion smiled. 'Now, since we're about to spend the evening together at your connivance, you must allow me to introduce myself. My name is Alexandros Faradaxis.'

'Kyrie Faradaxis...' Unnerved by his sheer animal magnetism as he regarded her with ironic amusement, she sprang into defence.

'Alexos, please,' he interrupted her smoothly. 'Since we are about to do business together.'

'Oh, but we're not!' That was an idea she would quash immediately. 'Neither do I intend to spend the evening with you. You must know the only reason I intervened was to prevent your making trouble. It so happens that an exception is made to the rule where I'm concerned. Because I represent a tour company and have a room in the hotel, I'm allowed to entertain Greek business contacts here.' She allowed herself a small smile. 'It's a concession to the fact that I'm a woman. However, once you've had the drink to which you consider yourself en-

titled, my interest in you is finished! You can take your
shield back with you to wherever it was you came from!'

'Meaning you regret your chivalrous action already,
agape mou?' He surveyed her pensively as she felt the
small hairs on the back of her neck rise. 'And that, far
from seeing me take my metaphorical shield back vic-
torious, you'd actually have preferred to see me carried
out on it—with your boyfriend's bar knife sticking in
my heart?'

She wouldn't have put it quite so bluntly, but he had
gauged her feelings very well and she wasn't about to
deny them. On the other hand, how dared he call her
'my love' in that patronising way as if she were under
some obligation to him, when the facts were reversed?

'I've already told you——' she started to remonstrate,
but he pounced on her words, distorting their meaning
before she could finish the sentence.

'That Manolis isn't your boyfriend?' He nodded complacently. 'I remember. Do you have a boyfriend?'

'Not now.' The words were out before she realised it
had been an impertinent question which she should have
ignored. Aware of the look of satisfaction which had
settled on Alexos's face, she turned her head away from
him, furious with her own loss of control. Of course, it
was because Philip's change of heart was so recent and
had taken her so much by surprise that she hadn't even
begun to come to terms with it. But still...

She bit her lip, glad that the moment of stress was
alleviated by the arrival of their drinks.

'A Greek boy, was he?' Alexos Faradaxis waited until
Manolis had withdrawn before asking the casual
question.

'English,' she said tersely, unwilling to augment his opinion of northern European women. 'Look, I really don't want to discuss my personal affairs.'

'We'll talk about something else, then.' He drained the glass in his hand before setting it down on the table. 'What do you suggest—boat trips?'

'Why? Do you have a boat for hire?' she countered briskly, hating the mocking smirk on his expressive mouth.

His response was a shrug. 'It would be easy enough to arrange.'

'Fine. If you've got any useful contacts, I'll certainly take their names.' She reached for her handbag, but was stopped as his hand closed on her arm.

'I'll work on the idea later. At the moment I fancy another drink. Will you join me?'

'Certainly not.' She shook off his restraining hand, rising to her feet with icy deliberation. 'I have no intention of staying here while you drink the night away. I suggest that now you've made your point you accept victory gracefully and look for some other bar where you'll be more welcome.'

'But I feel very welcome here.' Wine-dark eyes regarded her with considered coolness as they dwelt on her tensed figure. 'You might just as well sit down again, *agape mou*. You know as well as I that, having guaranteed my presence, you can't just walk out and leave me here alone. And you surely don't expect Manolis to throw me out after the lies you told, do you?'

Curse the persistence of the man! For a moment Ilona hesitated, torn between her need to escape and a natural caution, which told her that she was in danger of jeopardising the good relationship she currently held with the hotel management. The tour company for which she worked had considered themselves very fortunate in obtaining sole agency in the UK for the excellent El Greco hotel, newly built on one of the lonelier locations of Crete's north-western coast. It was essential she keep on good terms with the manager, who was determined to keep the El Greco's high profile unsmirched, if she wanted to continue living and working there.

'Oh, this is an impossible situation!' she said at last, letting her irritation show as she smoothed a wayward tress of deep golden hair away from her forehead.

'But not of my making,' Alexos said quietly, casting thoughtful eyes around their surroundings. 'I was merely looking for a pleasant setting in which to have a drink, and I find this suits me very well.'

'A taverna would have suited you better!'

'On the contrary, I was looking for something a little more sophisticated and it seems I've found it.' He nodded to the chair she had vacated. 'Sit down, Ilona Frankard, and tell me something about yourself. The night is young and I have a need for company.' He raised a lazy hand to summon the young waiter who had recently come on duty to assist Manolis.

Fuming inwardly, Ilona obeyed him, still uncertain of the type of man she had associated herself with, and unwilling to goad him into making more trouble. He was certainly striking to look at, his masculine bones incorporating a built-in hauteur of form and feature which suggested a heritage stretching eastwards beyond the frontiers of Greece, into the realms of desert nomads.

It was a bearing that would turn many women's heads, and probably accounted for his hubristic behaviour, she decided ruefully, regretting that he appeared to typify a kind of chauvinistic male with which to date she had had little experience of dealing. He was certainly not the kind of client whom one usually found on package tours, so it was scarcely surprising that her induction course as a courier hadn't covered the ground rules of coping with the volatile mixture of insolence and authority he projected!

His voice was low and cultured, and his English quite excellent. Also he had shown a good ear for linguistics, since he had guessed her mother tongue. She knew her Greek was excellent—after all, she'd learned it from Sophia!—but nevertheless he had been sharp enough to detect it wasn't her first language. If it hadn't been for his hands she would have guessed he was an entrepreneur of some kind, but those hands! Although they were clean and well manicured, the palms were hardened, the base of the fingers callused, suggesting a labourer rather than a man who lived by his wits. It was an anomaly that had already startled her as his skin had briefly touched the soft flesh of her arms. Something of an enigma, then, Alexos Faradaxis, and not easily to be jettisoned!

'There's not a lot to tell.' She shrugged her slim shoulders, making up her mind to humour him for the time being. After all, it wasn't as if she had made any other arrangements, and she would have enough hours of solitude in the months ahead to come to terms with Philip's desertion. 'As I said, I'm a courier, working here for an English tour company.'

'How long have you been here?' He relaxed in his chair, giving her all his attention.

'Just three months, since the hotel opened.'

'And how long do you intend to stay?' A dark eyebrow lifted questioningly.

'I'm not sure.' She made a small, helpless gesture with her shoulders. Since she no longer had anyone left in England who would be awaiting her return with eagerness, her future stretched before her, as bleak as it was blank. 'Certainly until the end of the season now, unless Happy Hellenic decide to replace me with a permanent rep. I originally agreed to come here as a temporary measure because they were desperate to employ a Greek-speaking courier. Until they made me the offer I was working as a clerk in their London office.'

'An Englishwoman who speaks fluent Greek?' There was a hint of amusement in his voice. 'A rarity, surely?'

'It's not a language on the standard curriculum of our schools,' she admitted wryly. 'But, you see, my maternal grandmother was Greek.'

'Ah!' He gazed steadfastly at her over the rim of his glass. 'That would explain your unusual colouring, *ne*? Eyes the colour of raisins, hair like fresh butter and skin as creamy as ewe's yoghurt...'

'So you're either a farmer or a chef?' She riposted tartly, not at all sure she was flattered to be likened to a recipe, even if it did sound like one for cheesecake!

He shook his head as a brief smile acknowledged her humour. 'Nothing so commendable. I take work where I find it these days.' Abruptly he changed the subject. 'Are you enjoying your stay here?'

'Very much.' She stared down at her own hands, surprised to experience a sudden need to confide her reasons for forsaking clerical work for that of a tour hostess. 'You see, Sophia, my grandmother, was born here, and I always wanted to see the places she spoke about with such nostalgia.' She made a small gesture of despair with her hands. 'She died about a year ago, so I suppose you could say I was making a pilgrimage to honour her memory.'

It had been something she had been determined to do, never suspecting how deeply she would be affected by discovering this part of her heritage, or how the dramatic, sweet-scented landscape would reawaken the poignant pain of Sophia's loss, just when she'd thought she had come to terms with it.

Alexos frowned. 'It wasn't possible for you to visit her while she was alive?'

'Oh, no! You don't understand. I lived with her in England. After she married my grandfather, who was English, her own parents disowned her, and she never returned to her homeland.'

'And your parents?' He frowned.

For a moment she hesitated. What on earth was she doing, spilling out her life history to a stranger in a bar? Perhaps it was precisely because he was a stranger and she need never see him again that she was finding it so easy to pour out the details of her background. Now that Philip had broken off their engagement she had no close confidant to whom she could turn for comfort, and there was something oddly compelling about her companion's interrogation, as if he was truly interested to know more about her. It wasn't likely that she would be offered such an opportunity for catharsis again in the near future, she realised ruefully. Happy Hellenic didn't encourage their couriers to have anything but a strictly professional relationship with their clients, and as for her fellow couriers... Well, in her isolated position, contact with them was rare, and Kate, the head representative in Iraklion, had shown no signs of befriending her.

What harm would there be in answering Alexos's questions? They had to talk about something if she was to keep up the illusion of a business meeting!

'My mother died from complications following influenza shortly after I was born,' she explained sadly, 'and my father went to the States, leaving me with my grandmother. When I was eleven years old he married again over there. After a few months he and his new wife asked me to go and live with them, but by then Sophia was more like a mother to me than a grand-mother...' She broke off, her memories of Sophia's death from a stroke too raw to be able to speak of it with equanimity.

Making a concerted effort to pull herself together, she was glad that Alexos had made no attempt to offer her false comfort, merely waiting silently for her to regain her composure. After a few moments she spoke again without distress. 'Sophia used to tell me so many stories of her girlhood that I couldn't wait to see the place for myself.'

'And you're not disappointed?'

'Not at all. Sadly, none of the family is still living here,' she confessed, 'but at least I've been able to spend my free time exploring the island and seeing for myself the sights that my grandmother used to describe so vividly to me.' She pinned a bright smile on her face. Since it seemed she was stuck with Alexos Faradaxis until he decided that he'd satisfied his honour, she felt the time had come to return the cross-examination. 'And what about you—do you live here?' she asked brightly.

'For the time being.' His answer was as curt as it was unforthcoming as he turned his head away from her to give his attention to a small group of musicians who had begun to set up their equipment on a raised podium in the centre of the room. 'Entertainment, too!' He returned his gaze to her face, a glimmer of speculation deepening the dark hue of his eyes. 'It seems my choice for an evening's amusement has been doubly blessed!'

Drat the man for his persistence! 'Are your family here with you too?' she asked sweetly, recognising and rejecting the gleam of sexual appraisal to which she was being subjected. 'Your wife and children?'

'No. My family live on the island of Kaphos in the Cyclades—perhaps you've heard of it?'

'No.' Ilona shook her head, experiencing a wave of annoyance that he should so readily acknowledge his personal obligations without a trace of shame for his present behaviour. But then, in her limited experience, many Greek men considered themselves answerable to no one, least of all a wife, where their personal behaviour was concerned! 'Should I have?'

CHAPTER TWO

'ONLY if you'd done your geography homework thoroughly.' The sparkle in Alexos's eyes taunted Ilona's ignorance. 'It's a very small island.'

If he was aware of her latent disapproval he chose to ignore it, continuing leisurely, 'Once it was a pirate's lair, but now it possesses a small town, a picturesque tiny harbour and numerous superb sandy beaches, and, since it has few roads and no airstrip, mass tourism has yet to discover it: but it suits my father and stepmother very well... As for my wife and children...' he hesitated delicately as if inviting her encouragement, and, when it didn't come, continued with a sigh '...in that area I have to admit to being a failure, although I was betrothed at the age of nine to the daughter of one of my father's friends on the island.' He shrugged powerful shoulders. 'Since she had only just been born and the wedding ceremony was envisaged as being on her eighteenth birthday, I didn't take the arrangement too seriously.'

His indigo eyes gleamed with amused self-awareness. 'It was a long time for a young man to wait for a wife and I'm afraid I sought consolation in other places, only to discover in the fullness of time that my betrothed had made her own plans, which didn't include me.'

'Oh!' Ilona searched his relaxed face, trying to read his true feelings. Had he felt the way she had when she'd discovered that Philip had found someone he cared for more than her? Surely not? After all, her circumstances were quite different. She'd been there in England with Philip, physically and emotionally close—or so she'd fondly imagined as they'd planned their future together.

A wave of pure agony forced her to close her eyes momentarily as the reality of Philip's betrayal pierced deeper beneath the armour of self-control she'd erected after reading his letter that morning. Had she been too complacent? Had there been warning signs she should have recognised before going ahead with the joint mortgage on a house? It seemed she'd been living in a fool's paradise, believing that Philip would be as loyal to her as she'd always been to him.

Now she was being asked to pay the price of her naïveté. Philip wanted to buy out her interest in the property that she'd been fondly thinking of as her future home. Having paid her part of the deposit from the small legacy her grandmother had left her, sadly she recognised that by itself it would never be enough to enable her to invest in her own property. When she eventually returned to England she would have to look around for somewhere to rent——

'One should cage one's birds first before leaving them too long to their own devices, perhaps?' The softly voiced question interrupted her thoughts.

'No, that would be wrong!' Quickly she contradicted him. 'Love must be freely given if it's to mean anything. You can't command emotion just because it's convenient!' She tore her eyes away from his intense regard, staring down at her hands, as the truth of her own words hit her hard.

For the first time she found herself analysing her broken relationship. Had it been based only on friendship and social compatibility, as Philip had alleged in his letter?

'Your philosophy is admirable, but not enough to hide the pain of parting, in your own particular case, *ne*?' From the other side of the table Alexos contemplated her face, his lips pursed assessingly.

She swallowed, the gentle question surprising her, because she thought she'd disguised the extent of her hurt well. A mistaken assumption if the narrowed gaze of her companion was anything to judge by!

Managing a slight movement of her shoulders, she attempted to indicate an indifference she was far from feeling. 'I've hardly had time to get used to the idea,' she retorted drily, wishing too late that she'd never started to discuss the state of her love-life with this disturbing stranger. 'Philip's letter informing me that he'd fallen in love with someone else and rearranged his future plans accordingly only arrived this morning!'

'Better a change of heart before the wedding than after, I think.' The unsympathetic murmur accompanied a sudden movement the other side of the table as Alexos rose gracefully to his feet.

'You're making a move, then?' Relief smoothing the lines of tension from her face, Ilona pushed back her chair preparatory to rising, prepared to be gracious now that her unwelcome ordeal was about to end.

'Not yet.' A dangerous glint sparkled in the depth of his eyes as he dashed her hopes. 'I was about to suggest that we dance.'

'Dance!' Horrified, she cast panic-stricken eyes towards the deserted dance area. 'Oh, no. I don't think that's a very good idea at all!' For the first time she became consciously aware that the normal bar lights had dimmed to allow a psychedelic display of flashing lights to play across the ceiling as the group of musicians began their repertoire of popular music. 'Apart from anything else, I can't cope with flashing lights—they put me off balance!'

It was nothing but the truth—all her life she'd been particularly sensitive to flickering lights, which at some frequencies had the unfortunate result of reducing her to unconsciousness—but it hid a greater one: she would be put even further off balance if she was obliged to put herself in the close proximity to Alexos that the current romantic music being played demanded.

There was no logical explanation for it but already she was finding his presence uncomfortably disquieting. It was as if, she mused, her whole body had become sensitised to his personal magnetism. Unless, of course, she considered moodily, the El Greco 'special' had been more potent than she'd bargained for!

'Nothing flamboyant, Ilona, I promise you.' Darkly persuasive, his gaze coaxed her as he smiled down at her expectantly, extending a lean hand towards her.

He really was absurdly good-looking, she acknowledged faintly, and just about the last thing she could stand this dreadful evening was to be held tightly in his arms, feeling the warmth and power of his lean body against her own. She wouldn't be used as a vicarious thrill by an itinerant Greek whom out of kindness she'd rescued from an embarrassing situation! She frowned slightly. No, that wasn't right! It wasn't Alexos she'd rescued but Manolis! Alexos was the villain of the piece and had already pressed his luck too far.

She sighed, not unduly surprised that he hadn't taken no for an answer. She'd seen from the first moment of laying eyes on him that he was a man used to having his own way. However, she assured herself firmly, he would hardly drag her on to the dance-floor, and that was what he'd have to do, because nothing was going to make her change her mind.

'I'd prefer not to,' she said firmly, still trying to evaluate his claim to being a bachelor. He wouldn't be the first man to deny marital obligations in order to enjoy the transitory company of another woman—or the last!

'As you wish.' Broad shoulders moved indifferently as she sighed her relief. Strange, though. She'd sensed an inherent ruthlessness in his demeanour that had led her to suppose he would have been rather more insistent.

'In that case——' she began confidently.

'Since,' he interrupted smoothly, as if he hadn't even been aware of her reaction, 'if I wish to dance in Greece I may do so without a partner.'

Her composure totally shaken, as her shattered senses confirmed that he wasn't joking, Ilona's mouth dropped open in shock.

'But not here...not now...please!' she hissed, her brown eyes deep and liquid with anxiety as she pleaded.

'Why not?' He was quite unmoved by her objection, his narrowed eyes like chips of sapphire, his fingers smoothing the pale shirt he was wearing against his tautly muscled chest. 'Don't tell me that you're unaware of our customs?'

'Of course I know the customs!' she snapped, trying hard to keep her temper in the face of such contemptuous provocation. 'I know men dance by themselves—and together—at the tavernas and nightclubs: but *not* at tourist hotels where Greeks are banned, and especially not to the sound of Spanish love-songs!'

The strains of '*Amor, Amor, Amor*' drifted round the bar as Alexos's lip curled in mocking derision. 'When a Greek feels like dancing—he dances!'

Flexing his shoulders, he began to move away from the table, his eyes still keeping contact with her outraged expression. He wasn't bluffing. As well as she knew her own name, Ilona knew instinctively that Alexos Faradaxis was quite capable of making an exhibition of himself, drawing the attention of everyone in that now crowded bar to himself and by so doing implicating her with consequent results that could damage her image with the hotel management!

With a feeling of sickening dismay she realised she had no option but to concede to his wishes if she wanted to keep her job.

'All right!' Her low voice trembled with frustration. 'Just one dance—and then you really will leave!'

Giving in to him was almost as painful as having to explain to a suspicious manager why she had chosen to flout the hotel rules would have been. Already she could feel her head beginning to throb, and, although the flickering lights would be partly to blame, Alexos Faradaxis's behaviour was by far the greater culprit.

'I knew you'd see it my way,' he said softly, his hold firm and supporting as he took her into his arms, guiding her towards the centre of the room.

For the first few bars she stayed rigid in his grasp, but the music was so evocative, the warmth and strength of his lithe body so compelling that after a while she relaxed against him. He was holding her close, but not uncomfortably so, yet she was frighteningly aware of his powerful frame as his cool hand on her back held her in steady contact. Hard thighs guided her unerringly in the simple steps that led them round the floor, and suddenly they were no longer alone as other couples joined them.

So close to him, Ilona found his presence even more impressive, her senses pleased by the aura of freshly laundered linen, the clean, sweet smell of sun-kissed male flesh and the elusive tang of a subtle cologne. She couldn't help noticing that his solid jaw had been newly shaved, but then, with hair of such velvet darkness, she supposed that twice-a-day shaving would be a necessity if he was to avoid looking like a pirate.

The thought amused her as she pictured him in her mind's eye with flowing-sleeved shirt, tight breeches and flourishing a cutlass.

'Ah, so you are able to smile, Ilona *mou*.' His deep voice caressed her ear. 'I was beginning to think I'd made a mistake after all, and you really did want to see the back of me.'

'I do.' But her reply was only half-hearted, as a familiar wave of nausea washed over her. She clutched at his arm. 'Only not at this precise moment.' She closed her eyes as her mental picture was replaced by jagged flashing colours. Placing the cool palm of her free hand over the shuttered lids, she winced at the excruciating pain, oblivious of everything save the need to escape from the source of her torment. 'I'm sorry, Alexos, the lights are beginning to affect me; I'm going to have to sit down before I fall down.'

As she stumbled slightly he caught her firmly round the waist, his voice harshening with concern.

'You were telling me the truth, then? You really are susceptible to flashing lights?' She couldn't answer, as even through her closed lids her sensitive retinas registered the irritating flicker, but she heard his deep growl of annoyance. 'I thought you were just being provocative.'

'No, I...'

She wanted to tell him that it wasn't part of her nature to be provocative, but he gave her no time to form the words, lifting her easily off her feet to carry her away from the floor and out of the bar.

Too giddy to worry about the impression they must be making on the other guests, she clutched at his shoulders, gratefully burying her face against his chest. Moments later she felt cooler air waft across her face and found herself gently lowered on a comfortable seat.

'Do you often get these attacks?'

She opened her eyes, already feeling the sickness and pain ebbing away now that the source of it had been removed, to find herself on one of the sumptuous settees at the far end of the hotel foyer, where it led to one of the entrances to the bar, with Alexos standing over her, regarding her with intent concentration, his eyebrows drawn into a contentious line.

'Not often,' she said truthfully. 'As long as I avoid discos and old silent films, I'm fine! It's a new group in the bar tonight and I didn't realise until too late that I would react so badly to their illuminations.' She dredged up a smile. Her exit from the bar might not have been all she'd desired, but at least it had removed Alexos Faradaxis from the danger area! All that remained now was to get him to leave the hotel. 'I'm beginning to feel a lot better already,' she said firmly. 'A glass of water and an early night and I'll be fine.'

'Very wise,' he nodded approvingly. 'I'll see you safely to your room, just in case you come over faint again.'

'There's really no need! It's just down the corridor.' Without thinking, she nodded in its direction, only to regret her outspokenness as he offered her his hand.

'No problem, then.'

For a fraction of a second she hesitated, but the door was only a few yards away, down a short passage, tucked in behind two utility-rooms. Small but a sufficient base for her operations, and at least it had its own bathroom. Apart from anything else, the thought of a cool, refreshing shower to wash away the memory of this disruptive evening was more than welcome.

On the threshold she turned to face him, determined to make sure he understood her position.

'Kyrie Faradaxis . . . Alexos . . . I'm truly sorry that the El Greco are so adamant about the people they'll serve, but please understand that this evening was an exception.' She drew a deep breath, regretting her previous loquacity that might have misled him as to her future intentions. 'I won't be able to sponsor you if you ever come back here again.'

'No?' Her heart flipped at his soft drawl, her pleading eyes discerning a cruel twist to the slow smile which curved his beautiful mouth. 'I think that's something we ought to discuss in a less public place, don't you?'

'There's nothing to discuss!' She felt in her bag, fumbling for her room key. Finding it with a sigh of relief, she turned it in the lock and pushed open the door. 'I'm sure you'll find a taverna which suits you as well as the El Greco and where you'll be more welcome.'

'Wait!' His hand touched her arm lightly but purposefully. 'At least let me put you in touch with one of my compatriots who will be pleased to offer you and your clients the use of his boat.' He smiled persuasively. 'He lives just off the main square. If you've got a scrap of paper I can draw you a diagram. I'm afraid he's not on the phone, but I can assure you his craft is spacious and well-maintained, and if you mention my name he'll quote you very competitive terms.'

'Well...' She hesitated and was lost. The pretext about boat trips had sprung to her mind in the first place because of the constant requests she was receiving from her clients. It was left to the resort representatives to arrange any such tours with local operators and she'd been trying her best over the past few weeks to satisfy their demands, but with no success. The small town was still unused to mass tourism and it seemed that the majority of boats were of the working category and not suitable or available for pleasure seeking.

Besides, it was a close community, and she was very conscious of the fact that she had not been accepted by the local inhabitants as anything but a foreign visitor: a person whom they treated with extreme courtesy but with no sign of warmth, a situation for which the inhospitable reputation of the El Greco had to take most of the blame!

A local contact would not only help her gain the confidence of the indigenous community but would also be a point in her favour when she asked for her tour of duty to be extended.

Taking advantage of her silence, Alexos crossed the threshold. 'Right! Do you have a pen?' He shouldered the door closed behind him as she took a few steps away from him, producing a notebook and Biro from her bag. 'It's quite simple to find.' He rested the book on her small dressing-table, choosing a page at random and making lightning strokes. 'Here's the main square, here's the road that passes the bank...then along here, down this small alleyway between the shoemaker and the *kafenion*. There's no number on the door—or at least there wasn't when I last visited it—but the man you want is Stavros Kiriakos. Just tell him what you're after and that Alexos sent you, and your troubles will be over.'

He passed the open book to her with a smile of smug satisfaction.

'Thank you, you're very kind.' Taking the book as he laid her pen down on the dressing-table, she cast her eyes swiftly over the diagram.

A careless wave of his hand dismissed her gratitude. 'Any action of mine pales in comparison with your own charity in befriending a lonely traveller in search of solace.'

For a few seconds she'd dropped her guard against him. Now warning bells sounded in her mind, stimulated to motion by the warm huskiness of his reply.

Uncertainly she glanced at his commanding face, one heavy strand of golden hair falling against her cheek as she shook her head reprovingly.

'You know that's not true,' she said quietly. 'I only had one purpose in intervening this evening and it certainly wasn't on your behalf. Now I'd be grateful if——

She didn't have time to finish her request that he should get out of her room, as he cut across her soft words, his own voice low in tone but vibrant with emotion. 'Do you make a habit of offering yourself to men and then changing your mind?'

The words struck her like a heavy blow to her stomach, depriving her momentarily of the means of answering him, while he stood there, sardonic eyes on her burning cheeks as she struggled for words, dismally aware that her action had been rash and open to misinterpretation in an island where many of the male inhabitants adhered to the tenets of a machismo society.

Warning bells rang too late in her mind. Alexos Faradaxis had been dressed in modern fashion, was obviously cultured and cosmopolitan on the surface, but she'd been wrong to believe he would accept her reasons for her own behaviour at face value! If it had been a mistake to accost him in the first place, she'd compounded it a hundred times by allowing him to cross the threshold of her room.

Miserably she acknowledged to herself that her usual caution had fallen victim to emotional stress, activated by Philip's unexpected and shattering renunciation of their relationship, increased by the unexpected potency of the El Greco special and reinforced by the hypnotic frequency of the lights.

With an effort she forced herself to meet the cool contemplation to which she was being subjected, a chill fear making her voice tremble as she dredged up the remnants of her pride. 'How dare you say I offered myself to you?'

'Didn't you?' The question was soft as silk, and she shivered, her innate femaleness recognising his brute strength and acknowledging how easily he could subdue her if he so chose. 'Do you deny you picked me up in the bar and offered me a drink? A complete stranger? It was a blatant invitation!'

'I do deny it!' Tears of rage gathered behind her eyes, but pride kept them dry in the face of his fiercely evaluating regard. 'How many times do I have to repeat that I did what I did for Manolis's sake?'

He laughed outright, but there was no amusement in the glittering glance that raked her from head to toe. 'You may repeat it a hundredfold and fail to convince me.'

'Oh!' She heaved in a deep breath, desperately searching for a way of escape from her predicament. If she screamed, no one would hear her, what with the disco in full swing and the remote location of her room.

Besides, one large hand across her mouth and all sound would be silenced. Yet up to now he had made no move to touch her, and, although he was undoubtedly far from pleased with her, he seemed to be in control of his emotions.

'I think that at worst you've changed your mind about how you wish to spend the rest of the evening. You have—what is the expression?—cold feet, *ne*?' He went on without a pause, 'Or at the best that you are trying to deceive yourself as well as me. Tell me, Ilona *mou*, if I'd been a spotty adolescent, would you have told the same lie?'

'No.' She winced at his choice of words, but she had to be honest. 'Because, if you had been, Manolis would have been able to deal with you. But you...' She paused tellingly as Alexos regarded her expectantly. Drat the man! Had she really been subliminally attracted to him as he claimed? But now was not the time to question her hidden motives as her accuser folded his arms across his chest and awaited her further words with an expression of taunting disbelief curling the corners of his prepossessing mouth.

'Yes?' He prompted her softly. 'What about me, Ilona?'

She raised her head defiantly, hoping he couldn't see the goose-bumps of apprehension that speckled her bare arms. 'It was clear that Manolis would come off worse in any confrontation between the two of you—both physically and verbally—because he was far from well!' Accusation was a sword in her large dark eyes as she challenged his *philotimo*, knowing the risk she was taking and praying she hadn't misjudged his basic code of ethics. 'You had the appearance and speech of a gentleman. I thought once your pride was appeased you'd behave like one—and leave!'

'Instead you discovered to your cost that I was *mangahs*?' He used a word which she knew was originally said to describe a particular Athenian type of ruffian, but had been taken into the common vocabulary to describe any man who was tough and swaggering, as he lifted a hand to imprison her chin with a gentle grasp.

It wasn't a word she would have dared to level at him, particularly in these circumstances, but her lips firmed stubbornly as she refused to deny his own self-incrimination.

He laughed with apparent good humour. 'I can salvage my own pride when necessary, *agape mou*. I don't need a woman to fight my battles.' His hand left her chin to wander to her hair as with a delicate touch he pushed a few straying strands away from her forehead. 'The truth is, you offered me an invitation that women have been offering men since Eve—and I chose to accept it.'

'No!' She tried to move away but the room was so small that her movement brought her up against the edge of her neat single bed and halted her progress. 'You were mistaken!'

'I *wanted* to accept it.' He stared down at her, his eyes narrowed, and she could feel the heat of his body and sense the burden of his frustration. 'It's a long time since I spent the night with a woman as lovely as you,' he said thickly. 'And now, having encouraged me to hope, you are planning to send me away unsatisfied?' A relentless purpose narrowed his eyes, deepened his voice to a growl. 'Or perhaps we can negotiate?' If he was aware of her look of horror he ignored it. 'If the business arrangement with Stavros is not enough of a reward for you—then you must name your price. I'm always prepared to pay well for the best in the market.'

Something inside Ilona snapped. He was too close to her, too achingly warm and male, his shoulders were too broad, and the promise of his strength and the hard comfort of his body were temptations that disgusted her. Anger with herself for the surge of physical desire which betrayed her mental antipathy towards him melded with outrage at his treating her like a woman who would sell her body to the highest bidder. Beyond caution, she swung her arm back and slapped his left cheek with her open palm, sparing no energy in making her mark on his lean face.

She saw the devilish glint in his dark eyes too late to side-step him as his hands seized her by the shoulders, effectively blocking movement.

'So you administer the punishment before the crime, do you?' he growled. '*Endaxi!*' His mouth lowered to take her lips already parted in preparation to deny him. Steeling herself for a near-violent assault, a bruising, punishing infliction of superior physical strength from an angry and frustrated man, she was astonished and relieved when his mouth took a tender, almost reverent toll from her.

To her horror she began to experience a wild, tumultuous joy in his nearness, which overlaid the shock of his action. In that moment she found the pleasure so intense, so sweet, that she couldn't fight it. Never in their entire time together had Philip kissed her with such contained passion. Never had her body responded to her ex-fiancé's caresses with such a sensation of joyous release.

She'd always known there'd been some element of excitement missing in their relationship, but she'd told herself that it was because Philip knew and respected the values her strict moral upbringing had given her. Because they both knew that, at twenty-two, she was still a virgin, she'd always supposed he had kept his lovemaking tempered to a level well below the point of no return.

How then, when she'd been only mildly moved by Philip's caresses, could she be feeling such a violent pleasure flooding through her senses as this angry stranger took his sweet revenge?

Confused and bewildered by her untypical reactions, she stirred restlessly against Alexos's hard body. Fingers that had stabbed uselessly into his arms at their first contact now lay still against the muscles she'd attempted to punish as his warm, insistent male mouth moved over the warm silkiness of her lips, conjuring a reply from deep inside her, seeking and finding a thread of desire that horrified her as much as it amazed her.

Dazed by his strength and purpose, she had no idea whether she'd returned his kiss or just let it happen. As his lips left hers she felt as if her bones had lost the power to support her. For a few seconds she leant against him for support, alert to the depth of his quickened breathing and the shudder that ranged through him, before he thrust her none too gently down on the bed, standing staring down at her, his indigo eyes accusing in the unsmiling hardness of his face.

'Just a word of warning, *glyka mou* ...' despite his mocking tone, a sixth sense told her he wasn't nearly as composed as his bearing suggested '... all men benefit from a mother's love, but it's up to their mothers to provide it. You are much too young and beautiful to go around "mothering" men like Manolis. It's not the kind of love an adult man appreciates—or even understands—from someone like you.'

Hurt by his contempt, Ilona swallowed painfully, trying to get a measure of control over her speeding pulse.

'You certainly made it quite clear the kind of love you appreciate!' she flung at him, embarrassingly aware of the tingling warmth of her lightly pleasured mouth and the warm tightness of her breasts beneath their light covering.

'Then you have received a lesson worth the learning, I think.' His condescension scorched her pride and infuriated her. Belatedly she searched the foggy depths of her brain for a suitable put-down, but in vain, as he swung away from her to open the door and vanish through it, leaving her to stare stupidly at its blank face as he closed it softly in his wake.

CHAPTER THREE

AWAKENING the following morning after a night of shallow sleep, Ilona groaned aloud as the memory of the previous evening flooded back to her. Stumbling from her bed, she made her way to the bathroom to stare with barely masked disgust at her mirrored face with its dark rings under heavy-lidded eyes. What a fool she'd been to intervene in a matter that hadn't concerned her! Her intentions of saving Manolis harassment when he was tortured by physical suffering had been good enough—but look where they'd led!

She shuddered, remembering how badly the handsome, arrogant Greek, whose acceptance at the El Greco she'd ensured, had misread her actions. It was just her bad luck that the new group playing in the bar had equipped themselves with flashing lights, she thought dismally. In no other circumstances would she have been so disorientated as to have allowed Alexos Faradaxis to escort her into the hotel lobby, or made the major mistake of thoughtlessly indicating where her room was located.

She frowned at her reflection. Even then she could have barred him at the threshold, but she'd allowed him to enter. Why? Absently she gave rein to her thoughts. The only excuse she could think of was that she'd been so shattered by Philip's letter that her customary caution had deserted her.

All she could hope for now was that she'd never set eyes on the impertinent Greek again! Surely even a man of his stubbornness wouldn't challenge the unyielding doors of the El Greco a second time?

A spasm of emotional pain tightened the muscles of her diaphragm. How long would it take her to come to terms with her broken engagement? she wondered. How long before this mixture of shock and grief faded to bearable proportions? She was an only child who had never known her father, and it was only now that she realised how much she'd relied on Philip to provide a male role in her life. A male role? Was that the loss she was mourning rather than the loss of a potential husband? But she had loved him, hadn't she?

Again the words indelibly printed in her mind surfaced—'I hope you will understand and be happy for me.' She conjured up his pleasant face, the hazel eyes and brown wavy hair, then turned away from the pale-faced image that mocked her trusting nature.

Showering before putting on a light make-up with a practised hand, she slipped into her neatly striped uniform dress, and made her way across the ground floor to the dining-room.

Had Philip ever really loved her? she wondered as she sat at her solitary table tucked away in the corner of the large room near the service entrance. Perhaps if he had he would have objected to her taking this job in Crete. She'd approached him tentatively, longing for the opportunity to see the land where Sophia had been born, but prepared to forgo the idea if he raised objections.

He hadn't, assuring her he could manage without her for six months. She took a deep draught of fragrant coffee. Fool that she was, she'd believed that he loved her so deeply that he was aware of the depth of her compulsion and prepared to humour her. Now she knew differently! Not only could he manage without her for six months—but also for the rest of his life!

At the time he'd told her that her absence would give him time to decorate and make the necessary repairs to their new house in preparation for the Christmas wedding they'd planned. Instead, as she now knew, he'd taken the opportunity afforded by her absence to fall in love with someone else!

She glanced down at her left hand, glad that she'd whole-heartedly accepted his suggestion that it would be an extravagance to waste money on an engagement-ring. At least she wouldn't have to go through the bitter formality of returning the token of his pledge to him! And there was no way she would have kept it, even if tradition had declared it her right.

Finishing her coffee, she made her way to the small partitioned-off area in the large reception hall of the hotel. With plenty of paper-work to do as well as making herself available for consultation with the agency's clients, she found that the morning passed quickly.

As the hands of the clock met at noon she gathered up her papers, and was on the point of thrusting them into her briefcase when she heard the extension phone in her small office ring.

'Ilona?' The slightly strident tones of Hellenic's chief courier in Iraklion sounded uncompromising.

'Yes, Kate?' Her heart sank. Not more problems, surely?

'Well, you've really put the cat among the pigeons this time!' Kate's sharp assertion justified her fears, but a quick check over events of the past week threw no further light on the matter.

'Is something wrong?' she asked pleasantly, trying her hardest to mask her anxiety.

'Only if you consider entertaining local Greek Romeos in your bedroom wrong! What were you trying to do? Turn the place into a bordello?'

'Oh, no!' Ilona wailed, feeling sick as she realised that the previous night's episode must have been seen by one of the staff and misinterpreted. Her fingers tightened round the receiver. 'Kate, please listen to me. It was just one Greek, and I didn't take him to my room. I came over a bit faint and he escorted me back there.'

'Tough! One or a dozen—it makes no difference. You're perfectly aware of the attitude there, and the manager himself has been on to us this morning, asking for your replacement immediately. He wants you out of the El Greco today or our contract won't be renewed.'

It was as if someone had thumped her hard in the solar plexus. Ilona gasped in shock. 'You mean I'm not even being given a chance to explain?' she demanded, horrified.

'What explanation's possible?' Kate queried ironically. 'Quite apart from one of the waiters being an eye-witness, you've already admitted you took one of the locals back to your room. I've spoken to London and I'm coming over to replace you temporarily myself. As for your job, the company's prepared to pay you to the end of the week and allow you to travel back to England on tonight's charter flight, but that's all. You've committed a serious breach of contract, putting their entire business with the El Greco at risk. As far as they're concerned, you're finished with Happy Hellenic—in any capacity at all! Is that clear?

'Yes, very clear.' It took an effort, but Ilona managed to control the latent shake in her voice, determined not to show her unsympathetic ex-colleague any sign of the devastation she felt. Events were moving with such speed that she was finding it difficult to collect her thoughts.

'Good,' Kate said briskly. 'You can get your own taxi to the airport and collect your ticket at the reservations desk. As you know, the flight leaves at six.'

As the receiver was noisily replaced at the Iraklion end Ilona sank down once more into the chair she'd just vacated, hardly able to credit what had happened.

She supposed she could have tried harder to put up an argument, but to what end? She'd been the victim of a cumulative series of events against which there could never be a successful appeal. It was *mira*, as the Greeks would say—fate, destiny, fortune. Predetermined and inescapable.

For a moment she considered phoning the London office herself and explaining the full circumstances, but realised almost instantly that she would be wasting her money. Happy Hellenic had their own problems, a small, specialist travel agency offering a service in a market that was decreasing because of increased competition and a recession in the holiday industry. The El Greco was of prime importance to them, since they held sole agency in Great Britain, and they knew, as well as she did, of the management's Draconian policies. Even loyalty to their staff would waver in the face of such adamantine principle.

But what was she to do? In a daze, she went to her room and started to pack. Where would she go if she returned to England? Not to the house that she'd been going to live in as Philip's wife! She shivered, despite the warmth of the day, imagining Philip's face and that of his new love if she knocked on their door: because how could she even think of it as partly 'her' door after what had happened?

A hotel, then—no, that would be too expensive. Couriers weren't paid very much and she hadn't got round to organising her own individual tours with the local people, on which she could legitimately make a profit! She laughed bitterly in the silence of the small room. Last night had been her first venture into such an arrangement—fool that she'd been! How Alexos Faradaxis must be laughing at her gullibility!

A room somewhere, then. That had to be the answer until Philip got together enough money to buy her out. Hopefully his beloved was gainfully employed and she, Ilona, would receive her just dues with as little delay as possible. But the interim prospect was depressing to say the least.

Finishing packing, she decided to spend the few hours she had left walking along the stretch of uncrowded beach facing the hotel. As she made her way along the soft, shifting sand she considered the alternative of staying in Crete. It was possible; but she would have to find work to support herself and, although she was prepared to turn her hand to anything, jobs for non-Greek nationals were limited, those that were available in the tavernas and hotels already filled by the regular contingent of northern Europeans who regularly made their way to where the sun shone brightest every summer.

Also she would have to find somewhere to stay in the interim. The cheap village rooms would all have been let to foreigners.

She paused, turning to face the gently swell of the ocean, deeply blue beneath a cloudless sky. This was the land her grandmother had loved above all other, although never returning to it after she'd defied her autocratic Greek father to marry an Englishman. Dear heaven! how she missed Sophia's fiery love and support, her understanding and compassion! Sophia, for all her strict code of morals, would have understood how she'd got herself into such a quandary and would have come up with the right answer!

'Oh, Yiayia,' she whispered, her heart full of grief. 'Tell me what I should do!'

'Teach your beautiful mouth how to speak the truth, for a start!' The voice so close behind her was as unmistakable as it was unwelcome.

'You!' she declaimed furiously, twisting round to face her tormentor. As if Alexos Faradaxis hadn't disrupted her life enough already! The last person she wanted to see at that moment was the man who was at the heart of her dilemma. Her jaw muscles tightened with anger. Dressed in white denims and a navy and white striped T-shirt, he displayed a casual elegance that was very pleasing to the eye. She made the judgement with detachment, convinced that her heart was hammering nineteen to the dozen not because of his physical appearance—only his physical presence; yet, seeing him again, she was inevitably reminded of that brief period of time she had spent held powerless in his arms while his mouth had flirted with hers and his body had dominated her.

Dark eyebrows rose above brooding indigo eyes.

'Yes, indeed, it is I. And I may not be your *yiayia*, but I'm sure she would applaud my advice, my beautiful little *pseftra*.'

'A liar! You dare to call me a liar?' Outraged, she took a punitive step towards him. He dodged it neatly.

'Righteous indignation sits uncomfortably on you lovely shoulders, *agape mou*.' Eyes as dark as the deepest Aegean caressed the complimented part of her body. 'Yesterday you told me you intended to stay in Crete to the end of the season, yet when I asked for you at the hotel a few minutes ago I was informed you were leaving Crete by the evening plane. So what's happened to make you change your mind? Has your lover discarded his new *philinada* and begged you to return to his love-nest?'

'Love-nest?' Bitterness scorched her tongue as she responded spontaneously. 'If you mean the home we were buying together, Philip has expelled me from that too, leaving me with no chance of buying a similar property if and when I get a refund of the money already invested!'

'Then if you were speaking the truth last night—why this change of heart?' he demanded sharply.

'Because yesterday I had a job!' she retorted fiercely, spilling out her frustration when logic told her that silence would better have maintained her dignity.

'And today?' He frowned, dark brows knitting as he contemplated her thoughtfully through black-lashed eyes. 'Are you telling me that today you have no job? Why?'

Resentment welling to flood proportions as her gaze dwelt on his dark, chiselled face with its arrogant air of interrogation, Ilona flared back at him. 'Because of you and your appalling behaviour. That's why!'

'Explain yourself!' The angle of his jaw tightened aggressively.

For a full five seconds she considered defying him. After all, there was nothing he could do to make amends. She'd brought the whole stupid misunderstanding down on her own head and she was mature enough to deal with the consequences.

'Ilona?' Two capable hands descended to her shoulders, one moving quickly to pinion her chin as she tried to elude him, forcing her to meet his enquiring eyes. 'I'm waiting for an explanation.'

Then he should have one, damn him! Drawing herself up to her full height, she faced him bravely, refusing to be cowed by his overpowering personality.

'One of the waiters saw you enter my room last night and, as the El Greco take a poor view of their premises being turned into a house of ill repute, my employers have been asked to arrange my removal forthwith. So I've been given the sack and sent home in disgrace. Satisfied?'

'No!' The vehemence of his reaction surprised her. 'Not only am I not satisfied, but I won't allow it!'

His reaction startled her. Somehow she'd supposed he would be indifferent to her downfall: regard it as a just penalty for her interference and the misunderstanding it had caused between them. Taking a long deep breath, she drew the warm, scented air into her lungs as the overhanging tamarisks on the beach-side walk stirred lethargically in the slight breeze.

'I'm flattered by your interest,' she returned at last, regarding his thunderous expression with a trace of amusement, her voice laced with irony. 'But I was unaware that you possessed Olympian powers.'

'But then, you know very little about me.' Beneath his burning gaze her whole body seemed to quiver with a new awareness. 'Since, as you say, I am responsible for what has happened, I will ensure you get another job, here in Greece. A job for which you are eminently suited and one that will ensure your continued source of income. That is what you would prefer, *ne*?'

'Yes, yes, it is.' Against all common sense, a faint flicker of hope was stirring. Anything would be preferable to returning to the loneliness that awaited her in England! 'But it's not possible to find anything in the time I have left.'

There was a minimal pause, then Alexos said softly, 'On the contrary, I have a solution that is both practicable and perfect. In a few hours' time I must return to Kaphos. You shall travel with me and become the receptionist at the new hotel that has recently opened there.'

'But that's impossible!' Wide-eyed, she stared up at him, while the tiny flicker of hope inside her burned brighter against all probability.

He shrugged. 'How so? What you don't know, you may learn. As I told you, Kaphos is visited by comparatively few outsiders, and very few of the natives speak fluent English. As most visitors have some English, your presence as an interpreter would be most valuable.'

'That wasn't what I meant...' She wasn't doubting her own capabilities of learning, only his authority in being able to offer her such a position. Yet despite her doubts a wild excitement was stirring in her heart. If such a job existed it would certainly tide her over until she could make her own independent arrangements; give her more time in her beloved Greece; save her from the ignominy of being sent back to London in disgrace...

'You don't trust me?' Alexos was frowning, correctly interpreting the suspicion that clouded her face.

She shrugged, unable to deny it, yet hoping against hope he could substantiate his suggestion. 'Do I have reason to? How can you know of such a job—or that I'd be considered suitable?'

His strong head went back as she voiced her distrust, and he laughed, the gleam in his eyes deepening. 'Because, Ilona *mou*, the manageress is a good friend of mine and was telling me only yesterday, when I phoned to confirm this afternoon's travel arrangements, that she was desperate to obtain the services of an English-speaking receptionist. It seems that Kaphos is too far off the beaten track to normally appeal to the kind of person she requires: but for you in your present predicament it could prove a safe if only temporary haven, *ne?*'

What could she say? The offer seemed too good to be true. Too good and too convenient, yet she was reluctant to let such a straw float past without making a token grab for it.

Her dichotomy must have been clearly mirrored on her face because Alexos gave another soft laugh. 'Once bitten, twice shy, eh? You think I mean to kidnap you, take you to my island retreat and make passionate love to you on a deserted beach where your moans of pleasure would be drowned by the murmur of the waves and the sighing of the breeze?'

Startled, Ilona wasn't aware of her slight change of colour. She *had* been thinking along those lines, although certainly not in such romantic terms! Put into words and accompanied by a sardonic smile from the insolent Greek, her fears seemed ridiculous.

'Of course not!' she denied the truth haughtily. 'But——'

'You prefer not to accept my word alone?' He didn't wait for her answer; neither did he seem too put out by her obvious doubts of his veracity. 'Very well, that is no problem. Come!'

She hesitated for only a second. What harm would there be in finding out how he intended to prove his offer? Giving a small shrug, she followed him to the narrow tree-lined beach road, accepting a seat in a tiny taverna at his request and allowing him to buy her a freshly squeezed orange juice. If nothing else, he owed her that!

Watching him invade the dark interior of the taverna, she wondered if she was insane to imagine for one moment that Alexos regretted his behaviour enough to want to make recompense, and—even more unlikely— was in a position to do so. Even if she could be convinced that she could earn a living on Kaphos, did she really want to be on the same small island as the presumptuous Greek, who would undoubtedly see himself in the role of her benefactor?

Before she could make her mind up he emerged, beckoning her to join him.

'I have the manageress herself on the phone,' he told her, thrusting a receiver into her hand as she came to his side. 'Speak to her. Satisfy yourself that she is overjoyed to offer you a job.'

Reluctantly Ilona lifted the receiver to her ear, uncomfortably conscious of the heavy thump of her heart against her ribs. So much could depend on the next few seconds.

In the background she could hear the comforting sound of children's laughter as a woman's voice confirmed that she was desperate to employ a reliable receptionist. The work would be light, day shifts only, and she would get free board and food plus a reasonable wage. It all seemed too easy. To be lifted from despair to this position of hope in so short a time was so implausible that conversely it had to be true!

'You'll arrive tomorrow with Alexos, then?' the soft, cultured voice at the other end of the line was asking. 'He tells me you're the ideal person for the position, and I'm really desperate to have some help.'

Licking her dry lips, Ilona drew a deep breath, conscious of Alexos's impatient presence at her side as he listened to every word. Faced with disaster on the one hand and adventure on the other, she fought down her qualms. Sophia had always told her that if she wanted something badly enough then she must fight for it—and she did want to stay in Greece for the rest of the summer...

'Yes,' she said firmly, aware of a sigh of relief on the other end of the phone at the same time as Alexos gave a grunt of satisfaction in her ear. 'Yes, I'll take the job.' Replacing the receiver, she turned towards her companion. 'What time does the ferry leave from Iraklion?'

'Ferry?' He lifted an eyebrow at her. 'What ferry?'

Confused, she frowned. 'The ferry from Iraklion to Kaphos, of course.'

'There is no ferry.' On the dark, saturnine face his smile was strangely threatening. 'Kaphos is much too small to warrant a direct visit from Crete. So, since my business there is urgent, I have arranged for a private craft to pick me up from the jetty in a couple of hours' time.' He gestured towards the end of the beach, where the grey stone walls of the small harbour were clearly visible. 'Don't worry, there'll be room for another passenger.'

'But I can't...' She stopped, biting her lip, irritated that she'd acted without finding out all the facts. She knew enough about the geography of the islands to re-alise that she was facing a night at sea. On the large ferry there would have been no problem, but on a small private boat? Just Alexos and herself and a small crew? Dear heaven protect her! Her recent traumas must have de-ranged her mind!

'Of course you can, Ilona,' he said smoothly, appar-ently reading her mind as easily as if it bore subtitles across her forehead. 'My old friend Aristide and his young son will prove competent and willing chaperons for you. Believe me, your virtue will be as safe on the *Athene* as it has ever been.'

His expression was bland, betraying nothing, as she stared suspiciously at him, seeking a hidden meaning to his soft rejoinder.

'Very well.' She nodded her blonde head sharply. She would have to trust him. Of all the options she had, it was the one she preferred. Yesterday he had misunderstood her motives. Since then she'd made her feelings quite clear to him, hadn't she? This was his way of recompensing her for all the trouble he'd caused. A reparation she most certainly deserved!

Besides, it wasn't as if she only had his word that a job awaited her. The manageress of the hotel on Kaphos had sounded charming...warm and friendly, and then, of course, there had been the children. The presence of children was doubly reassuring. 'I'll have to notify my ex-employers that I won't be taking up their offer of a flight back to England, and ask them to send on the money they owe me,' she said matter of factly, determined to take every precaution open to her before entrusting herself to Alexos and his crew. It was only then that cold realisation hit her. 'By the way, Alexos,' she asked steadily, 'what's the name of this hotel on Kaphos where I'll be working?'

Was it her imagination or did a shadow pass across his personable face? There was a moment of shattering tension when she thought he wasn't going to answer her very reasonable enquiry, then a slight smile curled the corners of his mouth. 'Belvedere,' he said lazily. 'Just—Belvedere, Kaphos, will be sufficient address to find you.'

As the *Athene*'s engine purred into life and she headed for the open sea Ilona stood by the rail on the sundeck,

watching the mountainous land of Crete recede slowly
into the distance. One look at Aristide, a man probably
in his sixties, and his early-teenage son, and her qualms
had dissolved. Perhaps it was because the male animal
at the extremities of age was a less dangerous creature
than the one in his prime, she thought, but more likely
because Aristide's face was honest and open, its texture
and lines a tribute to hard work and clean living, and
Timon's was young, eager and still innocent.

They'd greeted her with friendly respect, welcoming
her on board as Alexos's friend, and, although her reaction might have been simplistic, she had been instantly reassured, prepared to put her safety into their
hands for the coming hours, until she was able to rid
herself of Alexos's overwhelming presence.

'Impressive, isn't it?' As if her thoughts had conjured
him to her side, his voice sounded low and loaded with
feeling as he came to stand by her.

Turning her head, Ilona's eyes grazed his face, surprising a stillness on it as if it had been carved from
stone. Without the mocking smile with which she was
familiar, she fancied she glimpsed a sight of the real man,
observing a sombreness and depth of feeling that yesterday she would have dismissed as alien to his nature.

Was there really a sense of haunting pain clinging to
him? Or was her over-active imagination endowing him
with a sensibility he lacked?

Stirring uneasily, she agreed, 'It's very beautiful.'
Then, feeling a need to lighten the atmosphere by conversation, added a little hesitantly, 'Is Kaphos your real
home?'

'I was born and spent the first twelve years of my life
there,' he answered obliquely. 'My father and Calliope

live there permanently.' It wasn't a real answer to her question, only succeeding in confusing the issue.

Ilona frowned. 'Calliope? The girl to whom you were betrothed?'

He shook his head. 'My stepmother. My own mother died of peritonitis when I was three.' There was an aching emptiness behind his fine eyes as he turned to regard her enquiring face. 'There's no hospital on Kaphos, and by the time my father got her to the nearest island that could deal with such an emergency it was too late.'

Three years old! Ilona's throat thickened with compassion. She, too, had known what it was like to grow up without a mother's love. Sophia had been the best grandmother in the world, but she would always wonder longingly about the tragically fated Anastasia. Impulsively she laid one slim hand on Alexos's bare arm in a gesture of sympathy and understanding. Beneath her touch his flesh was warm and firm—disturbingly so. Quickly she withdrew her fingers, deciding that vocal sympathy would be a preferable expression of her sadness.

'How awful,' she murmured, ashamed at the inadequacy of the words.

'Mmm.' The indigo gaze raked her face. 'She was an English girl: dark, beautiful and vivacious, so I'm told; a student on a course studying Greek drama when she met and fell in love with my father.' He gave an odd little laugh. 'They met and married within the space of ten days.'

'English!' Shock coursed through her. 'You mean you're half-English?' She'd never thought of him as anything but purely Mediterranean in creed and culture, but all the clues were there... his height, the unusual blueness of his eyes...

'I'm no mathematician, but yes, that would appear to be the right fraction.' He was mocking her, amused by her air of disbelief. 'Now, if you will excuse me, there's something I have to check with Aristide.'

Taking her consent for granted, he moved to descend the short stairway, leaving her alone, head flung back, hair streaming away from her face in the breeze of motion, her skin tingling with the soft touch of spray and warm kiss of the sun.

CHAPTER FOUR

'HELLO, *thespinis*, you are dreaming?' Minutes later Timon appeared from nowhere to stand smiling at Ilona, assessing her carefree pose.

'Just thinking,' Ilona told him with a slight smile.

'Ah, yes, the funeral.' He nodded sagely. 'That is why you are going to Kaphos, *ne*?'

A wave of apprehension assailed her. 'Funeral? What funeral, Timon?'

'Why—that of Vlamios Jacovus.' He looked surprised. 'The godfather of Kyrie Faradaxis. That is why he is going back after all this time. I thought you would have known.'

'No; no, I didn't.' Fleetingly she wondered if Alexos's sorrow had fuelled his aggression the previous evening. A godfather played a much larger part in a child's life in Greece than he usually did in England, she knew; but Timon was staring at her with large, expressive eyes, as if doubting her right to be on the *Athene*, and she felt obliged to justify her presence.

'I'm going to work at one of the hotels on the island and, since Kyrie Faradaxis was returning there, he offered me a lift.' She smiled at him. 'It's as simple as that.'

'Hotel?' Timon stared at her as though she were mad. 'There's no hotel on Kaphos.'

'Of course there is!' She contradicted him with assumed conviction, but already she was experiencing a sinking feeling in her stomach. 'It's called Belvedere!'

'Belvedere?' Timon's face broke into a wide, enchanting grin. 'No, no, *thespinis*, it is you who is mistaken. Belvedere is not a hotel! It is the house which is owned by the *kyrios*—Alexos's father!'

Held immobile by an angry rigidity that seemed to turn her spine to steel as she uncomprehendingly stared back at the boy, Ilona felt the blood drain from her face. She'd been deliberately tricked—but for what purpose? 'A private house,' she whispered. 'There must be some other explanation!'

'There is.' Alexos had rejoined them, his feet soundless in deck-shoes, his voice deep and relaxed as he laid a hand on Timon's shoulder. 'Your father's got a job for you in the wheelhouse.'

'Then I'd like to hear it.' Scarcely waiting for Timon to disappear, she confronted her abductor, her face white with shock.

He stood facing her, his long, lean-hipped body totally relaxed. 'You needed a job at short notice and I was able to supply one.'

'But not in a hotel!' she countered, feeling her heart thumping painfully, despite her bravado.

'No,' he acceded gravely, 'at the house of my father, Theodorus Faradaxis.' The dark blue eyes fixed blandly on her face, alive with cool speculation, as he lazily awaited her response: a dangerous animal at ease, his power subdued, knowing she had nowhere to run.

'Why did you lie to me?' she demanded furiously.

A cynical sparkle lit his eyes. 'Because you would have refused my invitation if I had told you the truth. And because it was in both our interests that you should accompany me to Kaphos.'

'Ah...' her suspicions justified, her chin tilted upwards in unconscious defiance '...not pure altruism, then? So tell me, Alexos, exactly what kind of employment are you offering me? Does your stepmother need a maid?'

His cool, level gaze was unnerving as he returned her bold stare, and she was painfully aware of the pulse hammering at the base of her throat while her mind conjured up the intimate scene that had been played out between them in her room the previous evening.

'Not that I know of.' The timbre of his voice seemed to have deepened so that it was a growl of dissent. 'You should perhaps understand that it is six years since I last set foot on Kaphos. If it weren't for my godfather's death, it might well have been a lifetime...' He paused, and again she saw pain mirrored on his face before a quick blink of his dark lashes shielded the vulnerable statement of his eyes. As he paused momentarily she nodded her encouragement, controlling her own exasperation as she sensed the deep undercurrents of emotion emanating from him.

'The fact is, there is no love lost between my father and myself,' he said bluntly. 'For more than five years the gates of Belvedere have been closed to me, but even my father is not so uncharitable as to bar me from his house when I come to mourn the death of his friend and my godfather...' he paused, transfixing her with the intensity of his gaze before adding softly '...and especially when I am accompanied by the woman who has accepted my proposal of marriage.'

'*What*?' Recoiling as the meaning of his words registered on her dazed mind, she found her shoulders seized by predatory fingers as Alexos closed the gap between them. Unbalanced by his nearness, she found it difficult to keep her breathing steady as the fierceness of his passion communicated itself to her flesh through her light cotton top.

'*Akouse*!' His tanned skin stretched across the bones of his clenched jaw as he commanded her attention. 'Belvedere was where I was born. It was meant to be mine and my children's children. It is still my father's wish, as it was his father's before him, that there will always be a Faradaxis at Belvedere.'

'I don't understand...'

'No? Then I will explain. Calliope bore my father another son, my half-brother Nikos, but he has only two daughters and Frederica, his wife, is unfortunately unable to bear further children: so my key to entering Belvedere once more as a welcome member of the family is to discard the abandoned days of my bachelorhood and prove myself a reformed character. And what better proof than to bring with me my future wife?'

'No!' Sheer horror froze Ilona's tongue after the utterance of that one brief word. She wanted no part in this domestic quarrel. The moment the *Athene* reached the island she would get a return passage to Crete. She had money enough on her for that, and afterwards? She closed her eyes in despair at the blackness of the future that awaited her.

'A pretence for a few weeks only.' Alexos's strong male hands moved convulsively against her shoulder-blades, drawing her inexorably closer to his body, despite her attempt to resist him, his urgency compelling. 'A holiday in the sun, during which time I will reimburse you for your trouble, as arranged, while I find you a suitable job on another island. Is that so bad a prospect?'

'As arranged!' She confronted him furiously. 'Yes, you tricked me very nicely with your phone call to the "manageress" of Belvedere, didn't you? Since the lady was so ready to lie on your behalf, why didn't you ask her to play the part of your *arravoniastikia*?'

'Because she wasn't suitable for the role,' he returned coolly. 'Whereas you, Ilona ... You will undoubtedly be able to soften my father's heart with your innocent face and your enchanting smile.'

'And how will you explain the sudden departure of your beloved when the time comes for me to take up real employment?' she demanded stonily, mentally fighting the seduction of those warm, caressing fingers as they travelled their sensuous path along her spine.

His shrug dismissed the problem as unimportant. 'Time enough to think about that in the days ahead.'

'And then what?' She lifted an eyebrow at his lack of concern. 'Suppose you find the door locked behind you again?' She knew she should step away from his embrace but some dark force in his eyes made it impossible for her to move.

'If by that time I haven't regained my father's respect then I shall have to accept that there will never be a place for me again at Belvedere.' Anguish strictured his voice as Ilona's thoughts lurched crazily. He'd tricked her, but how could she shut her mind to such angst?

'Ilona?' It was just a murmur as his left hand came to brush the soft-blowing tendrils of blonde hair away from her cheeks. 'After all, it won't be the first time you have lied to save me humiliation, will it?' The touch of his fingers, their tips callused against her tender skin, started a wild pulsation somewhere deep inside her. Instinctively her own hand rose to still his.

'An impulsive action I shall regret till my dying day!' she retorted breathlessly, no longer troubling to protest her total innocence. Yet the realisation that perhaps he was right and that her sympathy for Manolis had been adulterated by some inner desire to preserve Alexos's dignity appalled her.

'Regret is a cold companion in bed for a beautiful woman,' he told her huskily. 'And why not be honest with yourself? You may find my actions repugnant, but physically you are not repelled by me, hmm? You are not nauseated by my kisses?'

There was no time to move, even if she'd wanted to, as Alexos found her soft, parted mouth with his own, taking it with a hungry passion. Her hands rose to repulse him and she shuddered, becoming aware of the contained violence that hardened his strong male body, the power of the muscles beneath the heated skin whose warmth encompassed her. But as his hands journeyed on her body in spasmodic adulation she found herself falling victim to the wild clamouring of her heart, unable to reject him, her dormant senses stirring in response to his potent maleness. Mortifying though it was to admit it, he had spoken nothing but the truth. Her mind might reject him and all he stood for, but for the first time in her life her mental control had ceased to transfer itself to her limbs.

He was breathing hard as he released her physically, pinioning her only with the hypnotic power of his beautiful eyes as she fought to come to terms with the ignominy of her surrender.

'Be realistic, *glyka mou*.' His mouth softened as a glimmer of a smile touched it. 'You can only lose by refusing my request, but you have everything to gain by playing the role in which I've cast you.'

'It seems I don't have any real choice, doesn't it?' she demanded coldly, regretting that she'd made him fully aware of the extent of her dilemma and confused by the surge of warmth that his kiss had conjured to rise in a tidal wave, only just beginning to abate, through her entire body. Why had she never felt like this when Philip kissed her? She'd loved Philip—enjoyed his embraces— but they had never wrought such havoc to her nervous system!

Somewhere deep inside her head a tiny voice told her she could escape the trap Alexos had set for her. She could explain everything to his father and throw herself on his mercy. In the circumstances, surely the elder Faradaxis would see her safely back to Crete—even employed?

No, that was impossible. Shivering as the *Athene* altered course and a stiff breeze brought goose-pimples to her bare arms, she realised that the price of any such revelation would undoubtedly be paid by Alexos himself. However imperious and ill-judged his actions, she couldn't bring herself to be the instrument of his final disgrace.

Suppose she did play a part for a few weeks? Gave him the opportunity to reinstate himself at Belvedere? Would it be so wicked to become the catalyst that healed the breach between father and son? Wasn't it an accepted aphorism that in certain circumstances the ends justified the means?

'Why not?' She said at last as he remained silent. Pleased with the light tone of her voice, she augmented it by giving a light laugh. 'After all, who wouldn't rather have a holiday with pay than work?'

'*Endaxi*!' His cry of triumph was accompanied by a mocking gleam in his remarkable eyes. 'I was sure you would see it that way eventually! *Ela, agape mou*, let us celebrate our betrothal in the customary way—with good food and wine!'

*   *   *

Morning light found the *Athene* at anchor in deep water off a small island, in sight of a picturesque harbour, backed by luxuriant vegetation, among which Ilona glimpsed clusters of whitewashed houses built in the traditional Cycladic architectural style. After washing in the tiny bathroom she dressed hurriedly in a dark mauve crinkle cotton dress and made her way on deck, to be greeted by Aristide and his son, both seated in the wheelhouse, the mugs in their hands betraying the source of the delicious smell of coffee that had awakened her.

Timon passed her a steaming mug. 'Are you going for a swim before breakfast too?' he asked.

It was only then, as she shook her head, that she realised Alexos was in the sea, swimming back towards the boat, using a slow, lazy freestyle, which carried him through the water with effortless efficiency. Walking over to the rail, she watched the smooth power of his arms as they hauled him ever nearer.

Reaching the side, he lunged for the bottom rung of a short rope ladder, lifting himself out of the water to clamber back on deck. Silently she picked up a folded towel abandoned on one of the chairs and handed it to him as he stood there, pools of water forming at his feet.

He was wearing bathing trunks, brief and body-hugging, and she couldn't prevent her eyes from lingering on his revealed near-nakedness in honest admiration. She'd been in his arms, held close by him. She'd sensed his power and the muscular superiority of his form, and last night, finding sleep difficult in the small cabin she'd been allocated, she'd wondered fleetingly, to her shame, what he would be like stripped. Now she knew. His body possessed a sculptured leanness that was breathtaking. From the golden-skinned breadth of his chest with the light dusting of dark hair between the

nipples his torso arrowed down without a trace of surplus
fat to a narrow waist and flat abdomen.

Hardly aware of what she was doing, her gaze travelled down his body, taking an aesthetic pleasure in the
natural balance of bone and muscle, which hadn't been
abused by overeating or drinking too much, or neglected
by lack of exercise. Because he was vigorously towelling
his hair, she allowed her eyes to dwell on the corded
planes of his torso longer than she would otherwise have
dared, noting how just above the band of his trunks a
fine line of body hair began, its darkness echoed on the
long, curving muscular thighs and calves of his legs—a
fine, silky coat, not thick enough to prevent the sun from
reaching the smooth skin beneath it.

She must be mad to engage in any subterfuge with a
man like this! Especially one that involved the pretence
of a forthcoming wedding!

'Having second thoughts, Ilona?'

His soft question brought the hot blood to her cheeks,
embarrassment overwhelming her as she realised he had
finished drying his hair and was standing, towel in hand,
regarding her with narrowed eyes.

'I'm not sure I can carry the deception through,' she
returned honestly, all her scattered reservations seeming
to gather force at his question to become an insur-
mountable obstacle. 'Apart from anything else, I don't
know enough about you to act realistically.' Her fingers
twisted the soft mauve cotton of her skirt. 'What do you
do for a living? Why is there this feud between you and
your father? How long am I supposed to have known
you? Where did we meet...?' Her voice faltered to a
standstill as she shrugged despairingly. They were all the
questions she should have asked him yesterday but had
still been too stunned to raise.

'*Arketa*!' he interrupted her hesitant phrases with quiet determination. 'I have every intention that we shall get to know each other better over breakfast.'

Feeling as if she was no longer in control of her own destiny, she capitulated, allowing him to lead her to the table already prepared on the sun-deck. But it wasn't until after they'd finished a meal of rolls and butter with thick peach jam and slices of Madeira cake that he broke the uneasy silence.

'My father has a large stake in Faradaxis Construction,' he began as she politely refused more coffee, 'a building company he started with his friend Vlamios Jacovus immediately after the end of the Second World War. About twenty years ago Vlamios sold his interest and with the capital financed a small but highly specialised boat-building company on Kaphos, catering for the tastes of wealthy and knowledgeable clients who wanted their crafts' performances to be as excellent as their appearance.'

He paused to take a long draught from his own coffee-cup. 'My father assumed that, as the eldest son, I would become a part of Faradaxis Construction, but as far as I was concerned not only would he have been impossible to work for, but also by the time I returned from my national service all I wanted to do was join Vlamios at the boatyard.' He paused, and Ilona encouraged him with a movement of her blonde head.

'What happened?'

'My father was furious,' he admitted. 'You see, my half-brother Nikos was only sixteen at the time and still away at school. It would be years before he'd complete his education and national service and be available to add the name of another Faradaxis to the payroll.'

'And that's what the feud is about? After all that time there's been no olive-branch offered between the two of you?' Aghast, Ilona stared at his unresponsive face. 'What is it that's kept you apart? Pride?'

'One of the ingredients, no doubt,' he allowed coolly. 'But, just as it takes two to quarrel, it takes two to make amends; besides...'

His pause was for so long, his darkly blue eyes so far-distanced, that Ilona fancied he was staring into his past—a past that contained all the elements of a classical Greek drama.

'Besides...?' she prompted gently when the silence became unbearable.

His attention snapped back to her, his eyes momentarily veiled so that their expression was unreadable. 'There were other incidents, too numerous to list, which forced us further and further apart.'

Deciding not to reveal the sudden surge of sympathy she felt for him, she said lightly, 'If your father is as terrifying as you paint him I'm not sure that a holiday with pay is sufficient inducement to persuade me to continue with this farce. I imagine he'd have no compassion for an impostor.'

'But he *will* have a tender spot for an English rose, even one so different in appearance from my mother.' His gaze moved assessingly over her delicate features. 'Believe me, I couldn't have found a better candidate with the whole of Crete to choose from, and as for payment...' He shrugged indolent shoulders. 'When I am welcome once more in Belvedere, that may be negotiable.'

His tongue was as smooth as his cheek had been against hers in the bar of the El Greco. Only now, she observed, his strong jaw was far from smooth, the dark stubble she'd anticipated lying beneath its surface in full evidence, giving him the appearance of one of the pirates whose ancient lairs had been on the island he claimed for his home.

Making an effort to draw her thoughts into a coherent whole, she said thoughtfully, 'It must be several years since you last worked for your godfather.'

'A small company like that must have a representative prepared to travel.' He stretched lazily: a large cat enjoying the sunshine. Beautiful to look at but dangerous to play games with. 'Rich businessmen are not always willing to take a long and tedious journey to locate an isolated boatyard.'

'Oh, I see.'

How stupid of her to assume that his contribution to his godfather's business had been manual, when he obviously possessed scholarship and ambition: but then, she'd been misled by his callused palms. A silly hurdle over which to founder when his use of the English language demonstrated a far better understanding of its nuances than an unaugmented school course would have provided.

Unaware that she'd been staring at his hands, she was surprised when he glanced down at them himself, throwing his palms open and observing their roughness with a mocking twist of his lips.

'These intrigue you, do they? You wonder how I come to have the hands of a labourer? That is easily explained. For the past two years I've turned my back on the boatyard to fulfil my father's dearest wish, selling my body and soul to Faradaxis Construction, carrying their hods, wielding their spades, driving the JCBs with my own name stencilled on the side.'

'You mean you'd already started on a course to win his approval....?' Her voice tailed away as he laughed outright.

My father didn't know, nor would have cared if he had!' he returned tersely. 'The time had come when I needed to feel the fresh air on my face, the ache of muscles well used, the physical pain of being alive when the bread on my table was earned with the salty drops of my own sweat!' Abruptly he pushed his chair from the table, rising to stand with his back to her, gazing towards the small harbour that awaited them when the anchor was lifted.

Stunned by his vehemence, Ilona remained silent, watching the tenseness of his body, aware that he was fighting some private battle, the details of which were not about to be made known to her. After a few moments he turned, his expression more relaxed. 'I was working on a site not far from the El Greco when Nikos phoned me with the news of Vlamios's death. Aristide is a trusted employee at the boatyard, a friend from my youth. There was no problem in arranging for him to collect me from Crete and take me back for the funeral.'

'Nikos is at Belvedere too?' she asked faintly, trying to estimate the extent of the ordeal that awaited her.

A sharp affirmative movement of Alexos's dark head confirmed her worst fears. 'He and his family always spend part of their summer holidays there.'

So her ordeal wasn't to be limited to Alexos's father and stepmother, she realised with a sinking heart. The wider the audience, the more difficult her part to play!

'What's the matter?' Alexos's lips had tightened at her obvious dismay. 'Is it going to be so difficult to pretend that you love me in front of an audience?'

'Without adequate rehearsal, yes!' she snapped back, realising too late, as she glimpsed a knowing smile of awareness bring a glitter to his dark eyes, that he had deliberately misinterpreted her assertion.

'If I'd known last night how eager you were to improve your performance, *agape mou*,' he purred, 'I would have invited you to share my cabin when my own turn at the wheel had ended.'

'You know what I mean,' she said coldly, infuriated by the mocking inflexion in his voice, and even more cross with herself for having left herself open to his smooth retort. 'Your family are bound to want to know some personal details—where we met, for example.'

'In Crete, of course!' Dark eyebrows rose in mock surprise. 'What's wrong with the truth?'

'You can ask that?' Fighting down a sudden urge to slap the sardonic smile from his face, Ilona rose to her feet, her nerves stretched to breaking point. 'I hardly think your family would be impressed to know that you'd picked me up in a bar!'

'Correction! You picked me up!' He laughed into her angry eyes. 'However, the truth can be adapted. All my family need to know is that we met in the El Greco and fell in love.'

'In the space of one day?'

'Well...' he mused lazily, his eyes mercilessly intent on her accusing brown eyes, '...that's all it took for Theo to fall in love with my mother. Such an admission would do nothing but endear you to him.'

'Us, you mean,' she returned contemptuously. 'Just how far are you prepared to cheat to gain possession of Belvedere, I wonder?'

'In life a man has to play the cards he's given. If they're not good enough to obtain his heart's desire, then he must bluff.' Indigo eyes glinted into hers, reflecting the annoyance that sharpened the timbre of his voice. 'And now, Ilona *mou*, time grows short and I must dress suitably for the sad formality that awaits me.'

With a sharp inclination of his head he moved away towards the cabins, leaving her frustrated and unhappy, wishing she could be tough enough to assign Alexandros Faradaxis and his masquerade to the devil—and knowing, as *he* must, that it was not within her nature to do so.

By the time he reappeared the *Athene* had lifted anchor and moved towards the shoreline, berthing against a short wooden jetty. As he came up on deck Ilona's eyes absorbed the sight of him, the crisp dark hair neatly styled above the mid-grey jacket of his elegantly cut suit, the thin line of white shirt at his wrists; then she caught her breath, because the form might be one of a civilised man but the sombre eyes that regarded her gazed from the face of a pirate, the jawline still blue with the increasing shadow of unshaved hair.

'You find my appearance displeasing?' His hand rose to his jaw. 'It is one of our island traditions that when death robs a man of his friend he demonstrates the extremity of his loss by showing how little he cares for worldly appearance in the face of such tragedy.'

'I know,' she admitted a trifle sheepishly. 'It was just that for a moment the custom had slipped my mind and...' She stumbled, wondering how to explain that, after she had accepted his appearance earlier that morning, when he had emerged from the depths like some reincarnation of Poseidon, the contrast between his civilised dress and the face of a dangerous buccaneer had aroused feelings of near-panic in her heart.

'And you were facing the prospect of being kissed by a bearded husband-to-be with less than total enthusiasm?'

'Of course not!' Fiercely she denied that the thought of being kissed by him had entered her head.

'Then I'm flattered that your affection for me is in no way abated by my physical appearance,' he returned smoothly.

'I didn't mean that!' she began to protest angrily, only to stop as he interrupted her with emphatic softness.

'No?' The smile he flashed her lasted for no more than a second and never reached his eyes. 'But death, after all, walks arm in arm with life like a fully integrated and accepted member of society, does it not? Whatever you meant . . . be assured that tomorrow my overt mourning will be over and my strategy to regain my place in my father's house just beginning.'

CHAPTER FIVE

'WE CAN leave the luggage.' Alexos was casually dismissive as he helped Ilona disembark on to the small quay. 'Aristide will bring it up to Belvedere in his *tree-kiklo* later. Transport's very limited here, I'm afraid, in keeping with the state of the roads! Apart from the odd jeep and my father's Land Rover, two wheels, a donkey or a boat are the usual forms of transport. I hope you won't find it too uncivilised.'

'On the contrary—I find it quite beautiful.' Refusing to be daunted by his cynicism, Ilona looked around, absorbing the sights of the small, colourful harbour with its scimitar-shaped parade of tavernas beneath luxuriant palm trees, backed by rising hills of sweetly scented pines.

'I'm gratified.' Her commendation was rewarded with a lazy smile from Alexos, which nevertheless seemed to embody a challenging quality. 'As Belvedere is barely fifteen minutes' walk from here, I thought we'd go on foot.' His gaze dropped to regard her sensible shoes. 'I see at least you've learned something from your stay on Greek soil.'

Refusing to question his insinuation that her choice of footwear might be the only thing she'd learned, she contented herself by saying simply, 'Walking's fine by me.'

As they left the harbour with its fishing boats and passed along whitewashed alleys her avid gaze encompassed a few small shops selling local arts and crafts interspersed with tavernas and the traditional *kafenions*,

72

where the old men of the village sat sipping their Greek coffee, fondling their worry beads and occasionally playing backgammon.

The winding road mounted all the time, revealing more shops on the second level, but these, Ilona observed, were for local patronage: dark-interiored general stores, the muddled shelves of which appeared to offer a selection of goods as varied as Harrods itself; greengrocers, where tomatoes and peaches vied with each other in their lushness; the fresh bread shop with its traditionally blue-painted door from behind which emanated the most delicious smell of baking, and a pastry shop, its shaded windows displaying a variety of confections that, even so soon after having eaten breakfast, had her mouth watering.

Above the shops, wooden balconies groaned under the weight of cascades of hanging geraniums and carnations, while at ground level twisted stems of bougainvillaea, jasmine and honeysuckle clung to the rough-surfaced walls, while the air was pervaded with their scent, mixed with the sweet, spicy smell from the pots of sweet basil, which seemed to appear on every alternate doorstep.

It didn't take long before Ilona realised that at every step eyes followed them. Old men looked up from their worry beads as they passed; elderly women dressed in the black of continual mourning paused in the action of sweeping their steps or picking their herbs. Mothers shopping with their children turned their heads, not attempting to hide their frank appraisal. Even the few younger men they passed seemed to pause in their stride to cast a speculative gaze on them. Only the scattering of tourists and the children ignored their passage.

Although she was aware that, in Greece, to stare was considered to show interest rather than rudeness, Ilona began to feel decidedly uncomfortable.

'Not far now.' Alexos slowed his pace after slanting a glance at the increased colour in her cheeks. 'Perhaps I should have warned you that it's uphill all the way.'

'Perhaps you should have warned me that the return of the prodigal son would excite such pointed interest among the locals!' she responded tartly, unhappily aware that his statement could also be a forecast of the days to come.

'Me?' He assumed surprise. 'I was under the impression it was your beauty that was turning their heads.'

'Don't fool with me, *please*, Alexos!' Vanity had never been one of her faults. 'From the attention you're getting, anyone would think you were notorious. I'd no idea this feud between yourself and your father would be so obviously known!'

He shrugged, jamming his hands into the pockets of his trousers in a violent gesture that would have made his tailor wince. 'Kaphos is a small place. If one of her sons sins then the whole population becomes his judge and jury!'

'You make it sound as if you committed some unforgivable crime,' she ventured, alerted by the latent passion in his voice, but even then she was unprepared for what happened next.

'Perhaps I did!' he rasped, stopping by the side of a narrow deserted alley to pull her into its shade, trapping her against the flaking wall by placing a hand each side of her head and leaning his body towards her.

'Alexos!' Her throat tightened as his inky gaze bore into her. There was something deep and dangerous here that she didn't understand. An underlying passion that threatened her hope of a peaceful week or so in this idyllic spot until such time that Alexos decided to dispense with her services.

'But there's no need to be afraid of me, Ilona *mou*.' His voice seemed to leave his throat with an effort, husky and laboured. 'I promise you I'll never hurt so much as a hair of your beautiful head...'

One of his hands left the wall to caress the smooth cap of her hair as her heart seemed to leap into her mouth. Held in a magnetic field, incapable of moving, her gaze pinned to his pain-racked face, she knew he was going to kiss her, and that there was nothing she could do to prevent it. Nothing she wanted to do.

When his mouth brushed against her own she made no effort to withdraw, shivering with a wild anticipation as she felt the slight rasp of his beard against her tender skin. As the first tentative caress met no opposition he deepened the kiss, drawing her away from the wall, enfolding her in his arms, removing the last millimetre of space between them so that their bodies fitted together in a parody of the act of love, hiding no secrets.

'Alexos, no!' Gasping with shock at how easily her inexperienced body had leaped to life in answer to his heated arousal, as if he had plied her with some aphrodisiac in preparation for such an event, she pushed hard at his chest, demanding her freedom. Ashamed and dismayed by her unbridled response, silently she cursed herself for her momentary loss of control. If he'd really thought she was on the hunt for a lover that night at the El Greco, what on earth would he think now?

'What's the matter?' His narrowed eyes were like sapphire chips as he gripped her wrists, holding her palms motionless against his chest so that she was unbearably aware of the deep, steady beat of his heart, the glowing heat of his flesh beneath the thin shirt. 'If we are to convince my family that I returned penitent to the fold and am about to embrace domestic life with zeal and ardour then we must give them some evidence of that fact, *ne*?

'Not to the extent of giving public performances of our phantom lust for each other!' she flashed back, her mind reeling as she fought to regain her composure, unable to explain or excuse her own wantonness.

'Public, *agape mou*? His eyes mocked her. 'The only witness of our tender embrace just now was a small tabby cat lying in the shade of a hibiscus bush, and I doubt we would have shocked that even if it hadn't been intent on washing its face.'

Seemingly in no great hurry to release her, he continued to regard her hostile face with dark, deliberate eyes while she tried unsuccessfully to rescue her wrists from the strong imprisoning fingers that surrounded them.

'As for what you so graphically describe as our phantom lust, believe me, Ilona, there's nothing phantom about my feelings for you,' he continued coolly. 'And as for demonstrating to my family how deeply our emotions for each other run...' he paused reflectively while some dark force in his expression held her on tenterhooks '...if you can't manage the soft smiles and caressing expressions of a woman in love without a little coaching—well, then, we can always rehearse in private to add authenticity to your performance.'

'I'm sure that won't be necessary,' she returned quickly while he finally released her wrists, his eyes coldly brilliant as she took two hasty steps away from him. 'I imagine I can force myself to look sufficiently enamoured to avoid arousing suspicion until the time is right to put an end to this farce.'

'Endaxi.' Beneath his mocking gaze Ilona's whole body seemed to tingle. 'But, should the exercise prove too difficult for you, just remember I will always be available to provide evening classes so that you may improve your portrayal of an enamoured bride-to-be.'

She caught her breath at his tone, discerning a veiled threat behind the gentle words. Tender embrace, indeed! If what had just happened between them was Alexos's idea of a tender embrace, heaven help a woman who became the object of his unrestrained desire!

Masking her indignation, she fixed her gaze on his dominating face, oblivious of the slight pinkness surrounding her mouth and chin where the harsh hair-roughened skin of his face had abrased it. 'I'll bear your offer in mind,' she said, assuming a coolness she was far from feeling. 'Do we have much further to go?'

Dark eyebrows lifted in simulated surprise. 'A very long way, I should say, judging on your recent reaction to being held in my arms.'

He was deliberately taunting her; still punishing her perhaps for what he was determined to see as her unkept promise of two nights ago. She must learn to ignore his innuendoes; refuse to give him the pleasure of seeing her continually rising to his bait. In time she would learn to disregard the curious tension that seemed to thrum between them. Perhaps if she kept reminding herself that he was in her debt—and not the other way round—it would help.

'Ah, well.' She gave him a honeyed smile. 'You know what they say—it's better to travel hopefully than to arrive, but, as you were perfectly aware, the only destination that interests me at this moment is Belvedere.'

'Then relax—your hopes are about to be fulfilled. When we turn the next corner you will see it. Come.'

Relieved to be once more on their way, Ilona obeyed his peremptory order, following him back into the main street and around the sharp-angled turn. The road was dusty, the twisting path that led away from it climbing towards the crown of pine trees which capped the steep hills outlined against the cerulean sky, blocked by a white stone wall, which she gauged to be about three metres high. Approaching nearer, she realised how extensively it reached along the parched and serried earth upon which it was built.

'Welcome to Belvedere.' Pausing by a metal-studded, heavy oak door in the wall, Alexos turned to face her, his expression enigmatic. 'Are you ready for the ordeal?' His eyes held a brooding challenge as they raked her sun-warmed face.

Too late to be anything but, she acknowledged to herself philosophically as she gave a nonchalant shrug of her slim shoulders. 'If you are.'

The door swung open easily on the latch as Alexos stepped back to allow her to precede him. Tense with nervous excitement, she stepped down three steps and found herself in the cool haven of a patio.

Height and shade were provided by subtropical palm trees and pomegranates, while shrubby oleanders sent their heady perfume to greet her. Earthenware and stone pots overflowed with colour, while roses and geraniums sprawled in rainbow confusion in isolated beds.

Beyond this lavish display, the house itself was a symphony of cool white stone and arched windows with olive-wood shutters and doors, one wall covered by glowing orange campsis vine.

'Oh, Alexos!' she breathed, entranced, instinctively appreciating his love for such a place. 'How beautiful it is!'

When he didn't reply she turned to catch such an expression of nostalgia on his face that she felt like a voyeur at a very private reunion. As a shiver trembled through her she raised her hands spontaneously to rub her warm palms against the goose-flesh of her upper arms. Immediately Alexos's eyes were drawn back to her.

'Afraid?' he asked softly. 'I promise you, there's no one here who will eat you.'

'Are—are you expected?' She couldn't mask the anxiety in the question. She'd given him her word and she intended to keep it to the best of her ability, but it was impossible to shake off the fear that sat on her shoulders like a cape.

The place seemed deserted, still and silent in the heat of the morning, as Alexos moved his dark head in a motion of affirmation, and raised his hand to a wrought-iron lever on the door.

Somewhere inside a bell echoed.

Seconds later the door opened to reveal a woman in her late fifties, her rounded face still beautiful, her dark hair caught back into a chignon.

'Alexos! Oh, my dear, dear son... What a joy it is to see you again,' she cried, her voice choking over the last few syllables as her eyes filled with moisture. There was no doubting the love behind the greeting as she opened her arms, and Alexos moved forward into her embrace, bending down to her smallness so that she could press her mouth to each of his bearded cheeks.

Touched and embarrassed by the older woman's tears, Ilona would have retreated, but as he straightened up

Alexos's arm snaked round her waist, imprisoning her to his side.

'Not only have I returned, Calli,' he said softly, 'but I have also brought with me my future wife—Ilona.'

Calliope's large eyes widened with shock as her gaze flickered between them.

'Oh, my dears—I'm so happy for both of you!' There was no denying the genuineness of her reaction as she reached to embrace Ilona. 'This is wonderful news!' Her hands clasped together in her eagerness to impart her joy. 'And you've come to Kaphos to be married? Here, this summer? To put the past finally behind you and make your future home among us? Nothing would please Theo more!'

Oh, dear heaven! This was worse than she'd antici-pated. Before the older woman's enthusiasm Ilona wilted. What could she say? How could she act out a lie to this open-hearted Greek woman who obviously cared deeply for her stepson? In theory their intended masquerade had seemed fraught with difficulties. Now that she had actually met Alexos's warm-hearted stepmother it seemed unthinkable that they should attempt to deceive her, however short the time of their duplicity.

Desperately she turned towards Alexos as he ushered her across the threshold into the coolness of the wide marble-floored entrance hall, silently beseeching him to take the initiative. The very least he could do was ex-plain that they had no immediate plans to become man and wife.

Instead, to her horror, he caught her wrist, lifting her hand palm upwards to his mouth to plant a soft kiss against its tender skin, glancing towards his stepmother through the thick fan of dark lashes that shielded his deep-set eyes.

'It's what I've dreamed of doing for a long time, he said simply.

As a warm glow of satisfaction smoothed the lines from Calliope's face a pang of inexplicable remorse twisted in Ilona's heart. Alexos had spoken nothing but the truth—except, of course, his dreams hadn't included her.

'Then the darkness of this day is already a little lighter,' Calliope enthused.

'A sentiment I hope my father shares.' Alexos's mouth twisted in a wry grimace. 'Is he here?'

The dark head denied it. 'He and the other pall-bearers are already at Vlamios's house. I stayed here to welcome you and take you to them.'

'Ilona...' Alexos turned towards her, taking both her hands in his, his expression solemn. 'There's no place for you where I must now go. Be patient, *agape mou*. When I return we will discuss our future plans further.'

'Alexos! Please!' Annoyance brought a slight flush to her face. How dared he give the impression that things had progressed so far between them? Unless she took a firm stand at the start, in his obsession for Belvedere, he'd have her garbed in white and crowned with ribbons, following the wedding candles along the road to the church, before she knew it! Her heart lurched at the thought, her pulse bounding into double time, as her imagination fantasised... Alexos beside her at the altar... Alexos exchanging wedding vows... Alexos in her bed...

'Later, *agape mou*, later,' he crooned soothingly, his expression filled with a melancholy that it would have been uncharitable to consider completely assumed.

'Later may be too late...' she began, only to have her mouth sealed, her words swallowed as he placed both his hands on her face, lifting her chin and kissing her with a gentle but thorough passion. She was panting when he released her, more from anger than lack of breath, her face pink with indignation at the way he'd chosen to silence her.

'Alexos, my dear...' Calliope, who'd momentarily disappeared, came back into view, looking calm and beautiful in her funeral black. 'We really should be going...' She hesitated delicately, then turned to Ilona. 'Forgive me for having to leave you so soon after our first meeting.' Her smile was warm and genuine, causing Ilona's heart to sink even further at the thought of the deception she was practising. 'But I've just arranged with Maria for a room to be made ready for you, and beg you to treat Belvedere as your own.'

'Thank you.' There was nothing else she could say as Calliope slipped her hand on to Alexos's arm, preparatory to leaving the house. Now was certainly not the time to take her fellow conspirator to task...but as soon as he returned and she was able to speak to him alone... 'My thoughts will be with you,' she added politely, and watched as they left the house together.

Moments later she was being led through the different levels of the house by a young maid, to be shown into a spacious bedroom that would have put a first-class hotel to shame.

'Roses!' Delightedly she buried her small nose in the vase on the bedside table. 'How lovely!'

'Kyria Faradaxis thought you would like them.' The Greek girl smiled complacently. 'Your luggage has not yet arrived but I've been asked to serve you with refreshment anywhere it would please you.'

About to decline the offer, Ilona hesitated. It was a gesture of courtesy and hospitality she dared not refuse, however fluttery her stomach was feeling.

'A glass of orange juice in the garden would be lovely,' she agreed, and was rewarded by a deepening of Maria's smile as she left the room.

Walking to the floor-length windows, she slid open the door, which led to a small balcony, and, stepping out, found herself looking across the roof-tops of the small town to the bay. Remembering the short flights of steps she'd climbed between sharply angled passages, she realised that the house hadn't been built on level foundations but carved into the rockface, and was even larger than she'd at first thought.

Finding her way down to the ground floor was easy enough. This time she turned away from the front door, walking through a large open-plan room graciously furnished with simple but obviously expensive furniture, the floor of which appeared to be of polished marble slabs on which were strewn three large Greek-style carpets of exquisite workmanship. Through one of the architraves, which gave the room an air of almost Moorish splendour, she could see the part of the garden that had been hidden from the front of the house. Here the central patio was dominated by a delicate minaret of a fountain, the soft sound of its spray mingling with the musical notes from a windchime made of shells, which swung in the warm breeze.

She had only just seated herself on a stone bench beside the fountain's pool when Maria arrived, bearing a tray holding a jug of iced orange juice, a tumbler and a plate of assorted sweetmeats.

It was here that an hour and a half later Calliope found her.

'Ilona, my dear,' the older woman came towards her with hands outstretched, 'how terrible that you've been deserted on this, your first visit to our house, but a funeral was no place for you to meet Theo; besides . . .' she paused briefly '. . . in the circumstances it was better for Alexos to speak to his father in private first so that they could settle their differences before we all celebrate your happiness.'

'And will they?' Ilona asked, unable to disguise her deep concern. Suppose the whole charade was in vain, that Theo Faradaxis was not prepared to offer his son the shelter of his roof? How then would Alexos justify kidnapping her?

'They will, my dear, they will.' Calliope laid a calming hand on Ilona's tightly clenched fist as she seated herself beside her. 'The men have gone to a taverna to drink their last toast to Vlamios. It will give Theo and Alexos a chance to relax and open their hearts to each other. But you can be sure that, now Alexos is taking a wife, Theo will be prepared to let the past bury itself and welcome him back to Belvedere.' Tears shimmered in her soft eyes. 'The last six years have been a nightmare for all of us, but now . . . well, now Alexos has broken the silence between himself and his father, we can be a family again. Theo was so afraid that he would continue to live in the past . . . become a recluse . . .' She moved her head sadly from side to side. 'It wasn't what he wanted for his eldest son!'

Ilona frowned. Alexos hadn't exaggerated the extent of the rift between him and his father, then. Unable to dismiss a vague feeling of unease, she decided to prompt Calliope into confiding further.

'Were things really that bad between them?' she asked uncertainly.

Calliope's intelligent eyes were forthright in their appraisal. 'All their lives they've sparked against each other like two pieces of flint. It doesn't mean Theo doesn't care for him, if that's what you're thinking—quite the opposite.' She uttered a deep sigh. 'But his way of showing his affection was to drive him hard. Perhaps if Christina had lived it might have been different, but I had no power to intervene, although at times I wept for both of them...' She paused, her dark eyes troubled.

'Please, go on,' Ilona beseeched, eager to add to her scanty knowledge of the enigmatic Greek whose arbitrary actions had disrupted the even tenor of her life. 'Alexos has told me so little of his early life, and it will help me to know him better.'

'What can I tell you?' Calliope pondered. 'That Alexos was—is—a thoroughbred. Hard work and high expectations only sharpened him, which was what Theo intended. He used to say, "Demand too little and that's what you'll get—too little!"'

'And Nikos. Did he drive Nikos just as hard?' Impulsively Ilona introduced Alexos's half-brother into the conversation.

'No.' The neatly coiffeured head moved in negation. 'Nikos is different from Alexos. He's warm and generous and loving—a son any mother would be proud of. That's not to say he's any less of a man than his brother—only he's... he's...'

'Not as hard as Alexos,' Ilona finished drily, and received a sharp look for her efforts as Calliope denied her assumption.

'Hard? Oh, no. That's not the word. Resilient, perhaps.'

'Alexos is obviously very fond of you.' Ilona's eyes danced with laughter at her companion's overt resentment of the implied criticism of her stepson's character. However harsh Theo Faradaxis had been with his first-born, Ilona could see Alexos would always have an ally in his stepmother. Her heart filled with a warm surge of affection for the gentle Greek woman.

'I know, and I'm grateful for it. It's not easy to take over another woman's child and make his childhood a happy one, especially when a child is born of the new union. But Alexos never seemed to resent me, and he and Nikos were as close as blood brothers—although there are five years' difference in their ages.'

'Alexos told me that he lived here until he was twelve?' Quietly she encouraged her companion to continue with her recollections, her eagerness to learn more about Alexos totally genuine. From the start he had been an enigma, a challenge. One that she hoped to understand better before their final parting, if only to assuage her own curiosity.

'That's right,' Calliope concurred. 'Theo sent him to school in Athens then. Of course, he came back here for the long summer holidays. I wondered at the time if the break from home would make him any less close to Nikos—but it didn't.' She smiled in reminiscence. 'Nikos worshipped the ground Alexos stood on. I think he'd have lain down and died if Alexos had commanded it! But Alexos never took advantage of him, never belittled him or humiliated him because he was younger and so much more vulnerable.'

Well, everyone can change, Ilona thought ruefully. The days of Alexos's not taking advantage of the vulnerable were obviously history. Still, this conversation was giving her a valuable insight into his youth, sketching in a background against which she could re-evaluate him. Fifteen minutes with his stepmother and she'd know more about her *arravoniastikos* than she'd learned in the hours she'd spent in his company!

'And when his schooling was finished?' she prompted softly.

'Ah—he came back here at eighteen—a man.' Calliope's head moved sadly. 'And the house wasn't big enough to hold the both of them—him and his father!' For a moment she gazed into space, sorrow in every line of her face. 'It was a situation no woman could mediate in—yet I loved them both.'

'But why—why was it so bad between them?' Ilona persisted, hungry for more facts that would help her to understand the complex nature of the man for whom she held such mixed feelings.

Calliope raised one black-clad shoulder, then let it fall again in a gesture of despair. 'I must admit that Theo delighted in provoking him, in forcing him to challenge authority. It gave him a great satisfaction, seeing Alexos fight against the bit. It made Theo proud he had a tough, arrogant, aggressive son—but, of course, he couldn't afford to let him win, however painful the means he selected to beat him.

'So Alexos left home, refused to go to university, and, after doing his national service, came back to Kaphos, but not to Belvedere. He chose to work for his godfather in the boatyard.'

And now Vlamios had gone, yet another strong link in Alexos's life broken. Then there was the girl to whom he'd been betrothed ... Understandably Calliope hadn't mentioned her, but that had been another affront to his father, another rupture in the smooth fabric of family unity. Besides, Alexos hadn't remained working for Vlamios. For the last two years he'd been employed, unbeknown to his father, by Faradaxis Construction, using

his undoubted strength of body, but not the power of
his intellect, in the interests of Theo's company. Why?
Had he decided that this was his only way to salvation
before she, Ilona, had burst into his life and offered him
an easier option?

There were so many more questions she would have
liked to ask Calliope, yet she found herself strangely
tongue-tied. Then she heard the sound of male voices
and felt a sinking sensation in the pit of her stomach.

'Relax—he'll love you as much as his son does.' Beside
her, Calliope smiled and gave her cool hand a squeeze,
blissfully ignorant of just how disquieting that statement
was. 'In the short time we had together before we reached
the church Alexos told me so much about you... your
Greek blood... the way he fell in love with you at first
sight. Believe me, my dear, Theo will be totally en-
chanted with you too!'

Until the day the whole miserable pretence blew apart!
Unable to contain her nervousness, Ilona rose to her feet
as the voices grew louder and Alexos walked out into
the courtyard with an older man. Of course it was Theo:
she knew it instantly. In his mid-sixties, the Greek stood
six feet tall, his hair still as dark as it must have been in
his prime, his body taut and well-disciplined, sturdier
and heavier set than the man beside him, but still for-
midable. And the face that regarded her with an air of
critical approval had the same hard bones, although the
skin was lined and weatherbeaten to a dark mahogany
tan, and the growth of beard was heavier.

But it was Alexos who came to her, putting out his
arm and drawing her into his embrace, turning with her,
the palm of his hand hard against her waist, as he faced
his father.

'This is Ilona—the woman I mean to make my wife.' Darkly aggressive, his eyes bored into those of the older man, and Ilona felt his fingers tighten. 'She is, I believe, *pateras mou*, everything you admire in a woman—chaste and beautiful and obedient.' Her head whirling with a peculiar kind of apprehension, quivering in his hold, Ilona sensed the build-up of tension, could savour the challenge in the formal words with every one of her senses as he paused. Then his voice was softening, thickening, as if he were alone with her. 'Also, I happen to love her very much.' He dipped his head and she felt his mouth brush against her cheek.

Humiliated by the empty words of love, she was powerless to prevent him from drawing her closer to where his father stood. 'Do you welcome her to your house?' he asked simply.

The silence could only have lasted a few seconds, but to Ilona it seemed a lifetime. Poised between the two men, conscious of the stormy emotions running between them, she looked into the proud face of Theo Faradaxis, not flinching from the hard eyes that scrutinised her with minute analysis. If she had realised at the time that her agreement to Alexos's plan would have landed her in this kind of high-profile scenario, she determined silently, she would have chosen to return to England and face whatever misery awaited her with resignation.

However unreasonable his father had been in the past, now that she was face to face with Theo Faradaxis she felt ashamed of her role. And what about Calliope? Couldn't Alexos see how hurt his stepmother would be when their mock engagement was called off?

Poised on the edge of a dénouement, she licked her dry lips nervously, unable to find the words she wanted to lighten the blow. And then a sudden swirl of wind

sent the windchimes into a harmonious chorus of joy,
and Theo stepped forward and took her by the hand,
saying gruffly, 'You are as beautiful as you are brave,
my child. I welcome you to my house and my family
and pray that the future will give you everything you
deserve.'

CHAPTER SIX

'AND NOW, if you'll both excuse us for a few moments, I've just seen Ilona's suitcase being delivered and I'm sure she'll want to unpack.' Smoothly Alexos slid his hand beneath her arm as Theo relinquished her palm. 'Come, *agape mou*, I'll carry it to your room for you.'

Only too glad to escape from Theo's warm embrace, Ilona silently led the way upstairs, indicating her bedroom, opening the door for Alexos and following him into it as he deposited her case by the bed.

'Alexos . . .' She confronted him before her courage failed. 'I'm sorry, but I don't think I can go through with this after all.' Unconsciously she twisted her hands together as she tried to evaluate his reaction, her eyes scanning his watchful face for a sign of understanding, and finding nothing she could equate with such an emotion. 'I've never felt such a fraud in all my life . . .'

'You agreed.' His soft voice betrayed nothing.

'Yes! But under duress and with no idea what it would be like. I accepted your argument that to bring a girl-friend with you might persuade your father that you were about to settle down and make him more kindly disposed towards you, but I never expected your step-mother would be making instant wedding plans—or that you would calmly accept them!'

'You mean you're afraid you'll wake up one morning and find yourself walking down the aisle beside me?'

'I'm not joking,' she returned stonily, standing immobile just a few feet in front of him, some dark force in his eyes transfixing her as her fertile imagination gave substance to the bizarre situation he had suggested.

'Neither am I, Ilona.' His firm lips compressed, denying her any hope of leniency. 'You must realise how unproductive and unkind it would be to disillusion them immediately. When the right time comes we'll tell them that we've had a change of heart. Until then we keep up the subterfuge.'

He was being deliberately unhelpful: unwilling to offer her any understanding or sympathy. A small flame of anger flickered for a moment in her dark eyes as they dwelt on his set expression.

'And when will the time be right?' Her small chin rose challengingly. 'When will the truth be less "unproductive"? As far as I can see, you exaggerated your father's hostility towards you. He seems overjoyed to see you again.'

'Because he sees you as my salvation! Because he believes I'm doing what he wishes: because he thinks I have won the love of a beautiful and compassionate woman who can live with my past!'

Impatience brought his eyebrows together into a bar across his forehead. 'I've already told you that what I'm doing is buying time. Time to share Belvedere with him as a welcome guest and to build a firm relationship between us that isn't dependent on anyone or anything else. Walk out on me now and the whole delicate bond that is beginning to re-form between us will be destroyed!'

'And it doesn't matter if I feel trapped and miserable in the meantime?'

'Naturally it matters.' His eyes met her querulous expression with an intensity that was as piercing as a laser beam. 'The last thing I need is an unhappy *arravonias-tikia*. My father would think I'd been maltreating you.'

'And he'd be right,' she returned moodily.

Alexos raised an expressive eyebrow. 'You won't be leaving here empty-handed or jobless.'

'You think that's all I care about?' she challenged, hurt by his callous assumption that her scruples could be disposed of by hand-outs. Physical attraction was one thing—and clearly Alexos had no arguments with her appearance—but how much easier the whole situation would have been for her if he'd liked her as well!

'Not necessarily,' he said softly, too softly. Warned by the latent threat in the simple words, Ilona took two quick steps away from him as he continued musingly, 'Perhaps I can find a different currency that you would prefer, hmm?'

'Alexos, no!' His purpose clear, she tried desperately to evade him as with one swift movement he caught her in his arms, pulling her hard against his own tense body as his hands splayed possessively against her back, while his mouth took hers with an angry passion. His kiss was deep and intoxicatingly seductive, his strong male body imprinting its power on her shrinking form, even as his unshaven jaw abraded her soft cheek.

She fought with mind and body against capitulation, knowing that he could physically subdue the latter but that she could continue to oppose him with the former—if that was what she wanted. So how was it that without conscious volition her body responded to the questing passage of his hand as it moved with unexpected tenderness between her shoulder-blades, its warmth excitingly evocative through the soft crinkle cotton of her dress, and her thighs relaxed in anticipation of a pleasure she'd shared with no man—not even Philip?

Philip! That had to be the answer. The whole painful débâcle of Philip's change of heart was behind this absurd episode in her life. It wasn't that Alexandros Faradaxis meant anything to her, only that he had stepped into a humiliatingly empty void in her life. The fact that he was everything Philip had never been had nothing to do with it, had it?

'*Theo mou*!'

It was only when Alexos's voice, husky and thick, broke the silence that she realised her opposition had stopped: that her arms were wound around his shoulders, her fingers reaching up into his thick dark hair, entwining the glossy, springy tendrils between them. Scarlet flooded her face with remorse. She must have confirmed his worst opinion of her. Dared she confess the truth? That she'd been thinking of Philip and how lacking in passion their relationship had been? That her unbridled response had been only because her mind was elsewhere?

Quickly she unlaced her fingers, releasing him from their capture. Trembling and uncertain, ashamed because she knew he would misread what had just happened, she pretended to rearrange her hair as his sombre appraisal raked her confused face.

'Now seems an appropriate moment to give you this,' he said softly, reaching into his pocket and producing a circle of gem-set gold. 'My father insisted on giving it to me the moment we entered the house, before he'd even met you. That alone should convince you of the importance he places on our betrothal.'

Taking her unresisting hand, he slid a ruby and diamond cluster on to her ring finger, adding unnecessarily as her lips parted in horrified astonishment, 'It was my mother's. He gave it to her on the occasion of my birth.' He caressed the ring with the tip of his thumb as it encircled the slender stem of her third finger. 'You can imagine how deeply offended he would be should you refuse to wear it.'

'Oh, dear God!' Ilona's voice shook as she stared at the jewel, realising how her dilemma had worsened with this unwanted honour thrust upon her. 'What am I going to do?'

'Wear it, of course, unless you are totally without charity.' He glowered down at her, daring her rejection.

'I can't!' Agitation sharpened her voice. 'It would be like sacrilege. Your mother would never forgive me!'

'My mother's dead, Ilona.' He halted her right hand as she moved it to withdraw the ring. 'Nothing would please her more than that my future wife should wear it.'

'Your future wife, perhaps—but that's not me!'

'But it could be.'

Alarm pounded through her veins, a slow-building fear invading every fibre of her body, as his words penetrated through her confusion. Was this the taste of fear? This bitter, metallic taint in her mouth? He seemed to be staring right into her soul as he repeated fiercely, 'It could be, Ilona. Wouldn't it solve all our problems?'

'Yours, perhaps,' she countered shakily. 'But I don't have any problems.'

'No?' His eyes were like a whip, stripping her of a feeble pretence with one quick lash of perception. 'No family...no lover...your former love-nest, by your own admission, about to be taken over by another occupant, leaving you homeless, *ne*?'

How could she deny what she'd already admitted? Fixing her distracted gaze on Alexos's darkly brooding features, she could only shake her head despairingly as he continued evenly, 'I, on the other hand, can offer you and our children a prosperous and secure future.'

'Children?' It was like swimming against the tide, she thought despairingly when a surge of warmth spread beneath her skin as insanely she responded to the thought of being the vessel for Alexos's progeny.

A line formed between his dark brows. 'You don't want children?'

'Yes—no. . .' she stuttered. 'I mean, not unless their father is the man I love.'

'Philip!' He spat the name out as if it soiled his mouth. 'Forget him. He's in the past!'

Astounded that he remembered her ex-fiancé's name—surely she hadn't mentioned it more than once to him?—she hesitated. What good would it do to admit that since she had received his letter her attitude towards Philip had undergone a complete change? That, instead of being heartbroken, now that she'd got over the initial shock she was beginning to realise that they'd both had a lucky escape? Their relationship had been founded on surface compatability without passion, a comfortable association of convenience, lacking the spark to inflame either of them. Painful though the revelation was, she was gradually becoming reconciled to it.

It was not an admission she would make to Alexos Faradaxis. Better to let her arrogant Greek tormentor believe she still loved Philip than to let him guess the warring emotions of fierce antagonism and compelling attraction that he himself stirred within her. Painfully she recognised that Alexos was partly responsible for her speedy acceptance of Philip's departure from her future. Alexos's vibrant presence in her life, his touch, his concentrated attention, his proprietorial air—the haunting aura with its traces of mystery and tragedy that surrounded him—had revealed latent emotions she'd never known she possessed. Conscious that he was still glaring at her, she made a slight dismissive movement of her shoulders.

'You surely don't expect me to marry you just to get a roof over my head—and what about you, Alexos? Do you really want to marry a woman you picked up in a bar?' Deliberately she made her tone light, dismissive.

His tight smile grated on her nerves. 'I can't afford to be too choosy.'

'So you've sown a few wild oats...' She shrugged philosophically, deciding to ignore his unwarranted taunt. 'You keep harping on about your lurid past, but I imagine most virile men of your age who haven't settled down to domesticity have a colourful history. If a woman falls in love with you she'll overlook your sins, however scarlet they are.'

'Including the one that resulted in a prison record?'

For a moment the harshly uttered question stunned her.

'Prison?' When she recovered it her voice quavered. 'You've been in prison?'

'For three years.' The confirmation came without a flicker of expression, alleviating the set mask of his face.

'But why? What did you do?' Horror and pity mingled and brought a lump to her throat at this totally unexpected revelation.

Neither was Alexos finding it easy to answer her. Transfixed by the small twitching muscle in the hollow of one of his cheeks, she waited for him to find the words he sought. Fraud...embezzlement? Drunk driving? Evasion of taxes? What sort of crime would a man of Alexos's calibre commit? Nothing she could think of seemed credible. It was impossible to envisage his doing anything mean or underhand or stupid...

'What did I do?' He gave a harsh laugh, which demonstrated pain rather than amusement. 'Not to put too fine an edge on it—I was responsible for a man's death.'

'Murder?' She thought her heart would stop beating. Instinctively she reached out a hand, finding comfort in the solid support of a nearby writing desk.

'Not premeditated...' Beneath the tan and the dark growth of beard his skin seemed to have assumed an ashen hue.

'But who...why...how?' Her mind was spinning, the enormity of what he had said almost too horrific to contemplate.

'Who? A man; a stranger, a drunken tourist; why...?' His face was drawn, his eyes glazed, as if he would never forget. 'Because he was being offensive, making a nuisance of himself. How...?' He gazed down at his hands, lifting them slightly, staring down at them as if they belonged to a stranger. 'They said he'd died from excessive punishing blows to the head. As I said, he was drunk and therefore unable to defend himself. The contest, if you can call it that, was one-sided.'

'Oh, dear God!' It was a prayer, not an oath, as Ilona whispered it.

Swallowing in an attempt to relax the tense muscles of her throat, she tried to gather her thoughts together. Suddenly it was much easier to understand Theo Faradaxis's attitude towards Alexos; the horror and bitterness that had barred him from Belvedere.

Theodorus Faradaxis had seen his first-born son, his strong and beautiful heir, break one of the laws of God and society. With both the crime and the punishment, he had seen an indelible stigma stamped on the house of Faradaxis and believed his dreams of seeing a grandson playing in the gardens of Belvedere forever shattered... unless somewhere there was a woman who would see beneath the label of brutality Alexos bore and discover other finer qualities that would enable her to trust and love him... marry him...

Those qualities did exist! Instinctively she, Ilona, knew it. Knew it so deeply that even now, with his confession still ringing in her ears, she was finding it impossible to believe.

'It disgusts you, *ne*?' He was watching her reactions intently, his expression grim. 'Now you will understand why I wished to delay this moment when I should read fear and horror in your eyes instead of the honest light of battle, and laughter and perhaps... friendship?'

Curiously frightening, his voice slewed over her, awakening a dormant foreboding. Memories of their stroll through the town flooded back to her: the way the villagers had stared at him as if he were a visitor from another planet. Then she had supposed it mere curiosity: now she knew there had been a deeper, more sinister reason behind their regard.

'I—no—I...' She tried to answer him but found her voice incapable of the task, and all the while she tried to control her larynx she was aware that it was amazement she felt rather than disgust. That Alexos was capable of anger she had no doubt, but surely not the senseless, brutal anger he had described? Her face paled as she remembered the way she had taunted him at the El Greco with the accusation that he had been about to assault Manolis... and his furious denial.

Then there had been his assurance on the way to Belvedere that he would never hurt a hair of her head. His meaning now was poignantly clear. And she believed him. That was the oddest thing of all. Not only did she believe that she would never suffer violence at his hands, but she also believed that he could never have been guilty of such a bestial crime, at least not in the simplistic circumstances he had described. There had to be much more to the story than what he had told her.

'It's all right, Ilona.' His voice was rough at the edges, but he stood as proud and fearless as Lucifer himself, accepting his damnation as duly earned. 'I accept the way you feel. As it is...' He opened his hands expressively. 'I've made my bed and, as the proverb goes, I must lie on it. Alone, it seems—unless somewhere there is a woman whose eyes won't mirror her revulsion when I touch her, whose body won't shudder in horror when I hold her and whose mouth doesn't go dry with fear when I kiss her.'

She moved spontaneously towards him, drawn by the agony etched into the hard planes of his face, and compassion flowered in Ilona's heart. 'There will be someone...' Someone like whom Theo had prayed for... someone like her... The eyes that met her own were full of shadows. Impulsively she touched his forearm, willing him to optimism. 'Believe me, Alexos!'

'Could *you* love such a man, *agape mou*? Shall we put it to the test? Shall we see if you are still as responsive to my caresses as you were before?'

Bitterness laced his tongue as he pulled her into his arms to ravage her mouth with a fervour that brought a singing warmth to every part of her body.

It was a cruel test and one she should have refused to undergo, yet she became a willing victim, mindlessly responding to him as if in a dream, feeling his released shudder of pleasure as he crushed her softness against his own tough, resilient frame.

With a mounting sense of exultation she felt his hunger for her in every thrusting, exploratory adventure of his

tongue as he ravished the sweetness of her mouth. In
the void of her mind the memory of his shocking confession lingered like a malignant growth, yet her need
was not to condemn but to comfort, to forgive him because he could not forgive himself. She who believed
fervently that human life was sacred felt only pity for
the tortured man who reached for her in the blindness
of his own suffering.

Lifting her hands, she threaded them through the thick
darkness of his beautiful hair, glorying in the heat of
his body as it warmed her own through the thin cotton
of her dress. She was on fire, wanting to comfort him,
to draw him away from the dark abyss that haunted him,
wanting to love him... Love! She was shocked by the
realisation; stunned by the suddenness of what had happened to her.

But this couldn't be the real thing, could it? This overwhelming tenderness she felt for him had to be the
mother love for which he had mocked her. Yet Alexos's
response to it was far from childlike! It was impossible
to remain unaware of the scorching power of the flames
she had aroused in his vital, graceful male body; impossible to ignore what was happening to herself, either,
when every nerve-end fluttered beneath his touch, when
her whole body had become nothing but an aching
hollow demanding an as yet unexperienced fulfilment.

As the full realisation of how the situation was growing
beyond her control burst on her Ilona tensed herself in
his arms, forcing her languid muscles to rigid opposition, reminding herself that, despite his obvious desire
for her body, he didn't love her. He had made it quite
clear from their first meeting that in his eyes she was
nothing more than a mercenary flirt, and his proposal

of marriage had been nothing more than a cynical attempt to regain his father's approval.

Reluctantly Alexos's mouth left hers. Relaxed from the intensity of their prolonged embrace, its lines seemed softer and fuller, but the slow, beautiful curve was as perfect as ever as he touched it down her throat.

'You see?' He spoke in angry triumph as he allowed her to disengage herself from his hold. 'I disgust you!'

'No, that's not true.' Struggling to gain control over her breathing, she denied it. 'You took me by surprise, that's all. Of course it's a shock...'

What should she feel? Horror? Fear? Revulsion? Outrage? Probably all those things, yet instead she felt strangely calm, her mind flooded with compassion because for three long years he had been caged and confined.

He was a man of pride, *hubris*, even, but he also possessed the twin qualities of sensibility and sensitivity. Whatever dark road had led him to such a destiny, he would have trodden it with no foreboding of the tragedy ahead. Of that she was sure. Without proof or excuse or even explanation, she accepted his deep regret as an incontestable fact.

Shivering, she imagined the torture of mind and body he would have endured during his days of imprisonment. Small wonder he'd chosen to work in the open air on his release, straining his sinews and muscles in hard physical labour, enjoying the freedom of unrestrained movement that working in all elements must have given him.

'You don't have to pretend, Ilona.' Grimly his voice intruded on her thoughts. 'But now at least you know the whole truth about my six-year absence from

Belvedere. A year awaiting trial, three in gaol and two trying to come to terms with the after-effects.'

'Yes, I see.' She gave a small uncertain laugh as she prepared to wound her own self-esteem. 'I also see how my predicament must have been like the answer to a prayer for you. If I had a suspicious nature I might even suspect you of deliberately arranging for me to get the sack.'

'Then you would be wrong!' He glowered at her, his voice thickening as he went on, 'I had only one thought in my mind that night when I held you in my arms. There are many ways of describing how I felt—some more poetic than others.'

'Alexos...please, don't!' Colour flushed her cheeks as she made her protest. 'I know how you felt.' She had no wish to hear again his unflattering description of her behaviour.

'No, *agape mou*, I don't believe you do,' he returned softly. 'But there is a little Greek verse, well known in the islands, that describes exactly how I felt.' His indigo eyes commanded her full attention as he continued in his deep voice, 'When you came to me and introduced yourself I looked at you and the words of that verse overpowered my mind...' Quietly he quoted,

'Your lips are sugar, your cheek an apple,
Your breasts paradise and your body a lily.
Oh, to kiss the sugar, to bite the apple,
To open paradise and possess the lily.'

The evocative words echoed round the stillness of the room as he paused. '*That's* how I felt, Ilona, when I looked at you. *That's* what I wanted when we were alone together in your room——'

'Alexos...'

She breathed his name, embarrassment and a responsive chemistry mingling in her blood, making her pulse race, her heart hammer, as, ignoring her interruption, he persisted relentlessly, 'And that's how I still felt the following morning when I went back to the El Greco with the intention of finding you and asking you to meet me again when I returned from Kaphos after my godfather's funeral... and found you packed and ready to leave.'

'Alexos...' She whispered his name again, aware of the dryness of her warm lips and afraid of touching them with her tongue because his eyes were fastened on their soft pink curves.

'And *that's* how I still feel,' he finished, his voice low and intense. 'Which is why you had to know about my background, even though it meant I ran the risk of alienating you completely.'

'It—it was a shock... unbelievable...' That was the truth, if not the whole truth. The incredible knowledge that she loved him despite everything must remain her secret or she would find herself trapped in a one-sided union, desired but not respected; loving but not loved.

'Whatever your feelings about me personally, give me two weeks, Ilona. That's all I ask. For the sakes of Theo and Calliope.' Deep and steady, his voice assaulted her ears. 'Already I've hurt them too much. Give me the chance to put this situation right without causing them more pain. Wear my ring: continue our deception for another fourteen days.'

Two weeks of being with him, faking a love that was becoming only too real, while he acted the lover instead of the sexual opportunist he was. How could she bear it?

'And after fourteen days—what then?'

He shrugged. 'By then I will have found you a good job on one of the other islands, and we will think of some acceptable reason for ending our betrothal. A reason Theo and Calliope will accept with sadness but understanding. When the time comes a suitable explanation will transpire. I guarantee it.'

It wasn't particularly reassuring, but it was all he was going to give her at that moment. Still she hesitated before committing herself.

'As long as they don't start making wedding arrangements. I don't want to disappoint them.'

'No?' he asked drily. 'The only way you can avoid that now is to marry me, and I believe we've established that's an unrealistic proposition in the circumstances, hmm?'

'Totally unrealistic,' she confirmed stoically, her heart sore with the awareness that he would misread her explanation, believing the circumstances to be those of his past, rather than his lack of love for her.

A deep ache in the region of her heart, she watched his wide, passionate mouth curve wryly.

'Tell me, Ilona *mou*, how high a pile of gold would be necessary to overcome a woman's moral revulsion of my crime?'

'You expect me to be a spokeswoman for my entire sex?' A splinter of savage pain pierced her. He could hardly have made his opinion of her clearer—in his eyes she was a woman whose integrity carried a price label.

'For yourself, then.' His narrowed stare was daunting.

Anger surged through her, intense and unbridled.

'If I loved you, you could be a pauper and still ''buy'' me with a single rose!'

For the time of an eye-blink his gaze left hers to encompass the graceful vase that stood beside her bed, before he took a couple of lazy strides towards the door.

'Let us hope that the next man to whom you give your heart is a successful gardener, then.' He turned, one hand grasping the door-knob. 'I'll leave you in peace to unpack.'

'It will only take a few minutes. Where will I find you—on the patio?'

'Without doubt.' Alexos surveyed her, his lustrous eyes bright and assessing. 'Frederica went to visit her own parents and collect the children after the funeral, and my brother Nikos followed on later. By the time you join us they'll doubtless all be back here.'

It was a forewarning and one for which she was grateful, although she'd no intention of thanking him. After all, everything he'd done since their first meeting had been in his own interests, hadn't it?

'Don't worry,' she returned coldly. 'I shall play the besotted *gomena* to perfection,' and was rewarded by an expression of amused contempt.

'An unfortunate choice of word, *agape mou*.' His deep blue eyes gleamed with laughter. 'At last your commendable knowledge of Greek has let you down. The word *gomena* is a colloquialism that implies a woman who is easily persuaded to share a man's bed. A "lay", I believe is a comparable expression in English?'

'Which was why I used it, Alexos,' she retorted sweetly. 'Isn't that how you've always regarded me?' and had the intense pleasure of seeing a dark flush stain his golden skin before he left the room without another word.

CHAPTER SEVEN

IT TOOK Ilona a few minutes to unpack, unfolding and hanging her clothes with the practised skill of an automaton while her mind, still dazed by Alexos's revelation about the last six years of his life, dwelt on his proposal of marriage.

Pausing in her task, she considered the exquisite ring encircling her finger, aware that, however much its monetary value, its sentimental value outweighed it. If only her emotions were less confused where Alexos was concerned, she wished helplessly. If only his glance didn't burn her with the same ferocity as his touch! It was so easy to mock at love at first sight, to sneer at Romeo and Juliet, to be prosaic rather than poetic. Yet hadn't Sophia defied her family and her culture by marrying her handsome Englishman within weeks of their first meeting? Hadn't Theo Faradaxis swept his English bride off her feet within days?

Perhaps such romantic propensities were bred in the bone, she chided herself. In which case both her and Alexos's pedigrees carried such undisciplined genes! Except, of course, Alexos had made no pretence of loving her. He only wanted to fill the gap in his life that his own perception of his future had identified. Perhaps if he'd shown the slightest sign that he cared about her as a person...as a woman...would she have considered it? Frighteningly, the answer was yes. Closing her eyes in spontaneous horror at the realisation, she heard in her imagination his deep-timbred voice speaking the simple, evocative words of the traditional Greek love verse, and felt a surge of warmth consume her from knee to neck.

This would never do! A quick glance at her watch told her half an hour had passed since Alexos had left her. Good manners decreed that she should not be too tardy in putting in an appearance, particularly since she would be meeting the rest of his family. Hastily she rinsed her hands and checked her appearance before leaving the room. She had made a bargain with Alexos and despite her very active doubts she was prepared to keep her part of it.

Reaching the patio, she was surprised to see that its only occupant was Alexos himself, casually sprawled on a flower-patterned lounger, a tall glass of iced orange juice in one hand. Pausing by the door, she drew in a deep breath, mentally composing herself for the ordeal ahead.

'*Thios Alexos*, *Thios Alexos*! Guess who I am! Guess who I am!' Before she'd had a chance to move from beneath the shadow of the large canopy that shielded the back of the house from the harsh rays of the sun Ilona saw a small figure appear on the scene to precipitate herself towards Alexos.

Placing his glass on the adjacent table, he sprang to his feet as the body of the young child hurled herself at him. Dark eyes smiled up at him as the sweet unsullied mouth of a little girl about five or six years old demanded an answer. She was beautiful: black hair hanging loose round a face that was stamped with the proud Faradaxis bones, but it was Alexos's expression that demanded Ilona's attention, a mixture of indefinable emotions chasing across it as the child held out impatient arms towards him.

'Xeni?' he whispered so quietly that Ilona could only just identify the name as the child acknowledged his correctness with a vigorous movement of her sable head. Lifting her up into his arms, he repeated in a tone of wonderment, 'After all this time—Xeni!'

Her heart aching for him, as he held his niece with that special tenderness that all Greeks seem to extend instinctively towards their young, Ilona watched the little scene as the child squirmed happily in his embrace.

'Mama told me you'd be here, so I ran all the way so's I could see you first! Mama's walking because Rena's sleepy and wanted to be carried. Why haven't you ever come to see Rena and me, *Thios Alexos*?'

'Because I've been a long way away,' Alexos told her thickly.

'But you could have come by aeroplane like Papa brought us from Athens before the boat came for us,' Xeni remonstrated, putting her small hand against Alexos's cheek. 'Papa had a lot of hair on his face too, but he got rid of it when we were at Yiayia's.'

'Your mama never did like beards,' Alexos told her with a rueful smile. 'Tomorrow my face will be as clean as your papa's—I promise you.'

'Are you going a long way away again?' the light voice demanded imperiously.

'Not if I can help it, Xeni...' But his eyes were no longer fixed on the child because another figure had arrived on the patio. Slim and exquisite, she moved with the sensual grace of a Velázquez madonna, black hair knotted on the crown of her head, leaving a shining mane to fall freely down her back. Dark eyes glowed in a complexion of magnolia purity, and her wide smile revealed perfect teeth as she advanced towards Alexos and Xeni.

'Frederica!' Even before Alexos had spoken her name Ilona had identified the lovely stranger in her simple dress of navy silk. What she hadn't anticipated was the charged look that lanced between Alexos and his sister-in-law as she approached and lifted her cheek for his kiss.

Dear God! She must be going mad! Was this what love did for one? Conjured jealousy out of nothing? But it wasn't nothing. Every nerve in her body sensitised by what had happened between Alexos and herself, she recognised that the atmosphere was heavy with undischarged emotion, to such a degree that she felt a wave of sheer embarrassment overcome her.

On the point of fleeing back to her room, she hesitated. She was being absurd: reading too much into what was bound to be a painful reunion. Neither Alexos's half-brother or his sister-in-law would have emerged unscathed from the scandal he had created.

'Nikos tells me that congratulations are in order, Alexos *mou*.' Frederica's voice was as soft and gentle as her appearance. 'We are both so happy for you.'

'And you, Frederica—are you happy?' There was a wealth of hidden meaning in Alexos's soft question—or was it simply her imagination taunting her? Despite the heat of the day, Ilona shivered. One thing was for certain: Alexos had never regarded her, Ilona, with the caring intensity he was bestowing on his sister-in-law! If she'd ever needed proof that all he felt for her was an uncomfortable and unwelcome physical attraction—this was it.

Even from where she stood, silently watching the small tableau, she could see the radiant smile that transformed the Greek girl's face as she confirmed softly, 'Now that you're back in Belvedere where you belong, *kouniados mou*, my happiness is complete.'

Perhaps it was the shock of learning about Alexos's dark history or perhaps she just wasn't accustomed to such traumatic reunions, but to Ilona's ears the quiet, husky words hid far more than they revealed.

'And how is my brother? He left so soon after the funeral to collect you and the children that we had time for nothing more than a brief acknowledgement.' Alexos was so intent on Frederica that her own presence had been completely undetected. Perhaps she should return to her room, Ilona thought uncomfortably, poised for flight yet held in place by unseen bonds.

'Oh, Nikos is fine; much better, in fact. Not that he's forgotten what happened . . .' She glanced at Xeni's animated little face, and obviously thought better about finishing her sentence. 'Nikos is fine,' she repeated firmly. 'Rena went to sleep in my arms and, believe me, although she's only three she's no lightweight, so he took over the burden, which left me free to hurry back to welcome you home.'

'Here's Papa and Rena,' Xeni announced happily, seemingly unaware of the crackling electric aura entrapping her mother and uncle. Wriggling her way out of Alexos's arms, she ran across the patio to greet the man who was coming into view, a sleeping child held against his shoulder.

As Nikos Faradaxis approached, Ilona detected a definite similarity between the two half-brothers. The stamp of the Faradaxis line, she thought wryly. But Nikos's frame was lighter and smaller than his half-brother's, his step less positive, his head held less high.

'Nikos!' Alexos stepped forward, his hand extended.

For one awful moment it seemed as if the younger man would reject the offer of reconciliation as he met his brother's frank gaze then glanced away.

'Here, let me take Rena...' It was Frederica who stepped into the breach, lifting the sleeping child away from her husband's relaxed grasp. 'Then the two of you can embrace as brothers should.'

It sounded more like an instruction than a suggestion, her soft voice suddenly needle-sharp, and both men responded to it, clasping each other in the familial embrace of affection customary in Mediterranean countries.

Of course, she'd been over-reacting. An hour later, sitting at the beautiful oval table, sharing a celebration lunch with the whole Faradaxis family, Ilona admitted it freely to herself. Doubtless the strain of the last couple of days had begun to tell on her, firing her subconscious mind with all kinds of bizarre fantasies: that and the turbulent mixture of emotions which plagued her every time she looked at Alexos.

Of course, she lectured herself silently but firmly as she forked the delicious *keftedes* in egg and lemon sauce around her plate, any meeting between him and his sister-in-law was bound to have dramatic undertones after such a long time and in such constrained circumstances. Now, enjoying the excellent food and drink, she forced herself to relax, mocking herself for her ridiculous imaginings.

Nikos, after that first uneasy greeting for his half-brother, appeared to have uncovered a fount of high spirits, projecting the same easy charm that Alexos could conjure up when it suited him, and when she'd finally found enough courage to venture forth to join the small party on the patio she'd been greeted with the utmost courtesy: both Frederica and her husband appearing to greet the news of Alexos's proposed marriage with sincere approval, while Nikos had been almost boisterous in his acceptance of her into the family.

Dear heaven! How bad she'd felt at that moment of congratulation, finding herself hardly able to meet Alexos's eye as he'd placed one firm arm around her shoulders, drawing her towards him with suitable lover-like zeal.

Hopefully her awkwardness had been interpreted as shyness rather than stand-offishness. Certainly Xeni had taken to her readily enough, her childish chatter smoothing over any lulls in the conversation.

They were both delightful children, she accorded. Accepting a small helping of the exotic dessert Calliope had prepared in honour of the reunion, she recalled with pleasure the way both youngsters had amused themselves with her in the garden, after Rena had awakened from her snooze, while the rest of the family had settled down to renew their long-standing but tragically disturbed ties.

Three-year-old Rena was a docile child, content to follow the lead of her older sister. Not that Xeni was demanding, just that her character owed a lot to her Faradaxis genes! She was an amusing and intelligent companion, keeping up a torrent of questions, when she wasn't talking about herself and her school, until Ilona felt she must know more about the child than her uncle!

'That's a pretty name—Xeni,' she interposed into a rare gap in the conversation at the lunch table. 'I don't think it's one I've come across before.'

The child laughed delightedly. 'My real name's Polyxena because I was born five years ago on her saint's day, but everyone calls me Xeni—except Yiayia, who sometimes calls me Polly!'

'And your sister—was Rena born on St Irene's Day?'

Xena nodded enthusiastically. 'And Daddy was born on St Nicholas's Day,' she volunteered happily.

Obviously a family custom, Ilona decided, knowing it was a fairly usual one in Greece. She was about to ask if Uncle Alexos had also been named after his saint's day when Nikos commandeered her attention, looking over Xeni's head and pinioning her with his attractive smile.

'So when's the wedding to be, Ilona?'

As panic flared through her she sought Alexos's help with a pleading glance across the table.

'We haven't settled on a date yet,' he came to her rescue with consummate calm. 'Ilona's father is in the United States and unfortunately we haven't been able to contact him yet. Naturally she wants his blessing before naming a date.' He shrugged broad shoulders beneath his pristine white shirt. 'But as far as we're both concerned the sooner the better.'

'Wouldn't it be lovely if you could make it the twentieth of next month?' Frederica leant forward, her eager face focused on Ilona's. 'That's when Nikos and I celebrate our own wedding anniversary. We could have a double celebration!'

'Yes, six years of married bliss.' A shadow seemed to pass over Nikos's countenance as his dark eyes moved slowly over his wife's lovely face. 'But perhaps Alexos and Ilona prefer something quiet?'

'Ilona?' Alexos's hand snaked across the table to rest on her own as it lay idly beside her plate, his smile taunting her as his raised eyebrows invited her opinion, as if they were really discussing an event that was going to take place.

Damn him for his arrogant disregard of her feelings! But she had promised to act out the lie until he was ready to release her, so she forced an answering smile to her dry lips, amazed that he'd remembered that detail about her early life.

'I—I really don't mind. Whatever pleases you,' she offered simply.

'Then by all means, provided we can get your father's blessing in time, we'll arrange a double celebration.' Blue-black eyes demanded approval of his polished performance from her. Reluctantly she dipped her head, acknowledging it, tacitly accepting his apparent decision while inwardly congratulating him on formulating a plan to release her from her false position. Clever Alexos! She regarded his proud face from beneath her fan of lowered lashes. All that was necessary was for her father to 'disapprove' of their intended union and, acting the dutiful daughter, she would reluctantly withdraw from the commitment in deference to his wishes.

Neither would it be difficult for him to formulate a reason! she thought grimly. Not many men would want a criminal for a son-in-law! Not that Michael Frankard could care less about what she did—but that was something the Faradaxises wouldn't need to know.

'Splendid!' Theo boomed. 'We'll hire the biggest taverna—no, the two biggest tavernas in Kaphos, and invite the whole island to celebrate, a proper Greek wedding—good food and wine and plenty of it, and music and dancing into the night. We'll let the whole population know how proud Theodorus Faradaxis is of both his sons and their lovely wives!'

It was a moment of triumph for Alexos, and she shared it with him as he acknowledged his father's pleasure, raising the wine glass he was offered and toasting first the older man, then his half-brother, before raising it to his own lips and downing it in one swallow. She half expected him to smash it on the floor but he contented himself with replacing it carefully on the table, before changing the subject to enquire about the fortunes of Faradaxis Construction.

It was natural at that point that Theo should want to know more about her own background. So the children were granted permission to leave the table and the adults relaxed on the comfort of the soft upholstered couches as coffee was served, while Ilona spilled out the story of Sophia and her wayward love for the young Englishman whom she had chosen to marry in place of the Greek merchant preferred by her father.

Lifting her shoulders, she let them fall despairingly. 'After she defied her father she was never able to return to Crete. He made it quite clear to her that as far as he was concerned she no longer existed.'

'We do not give up our daughters easily to an outsider.' Theo's dark eyes dwelt on her sympathetically. 'It is not that we don't trust men of another race, only that we know our daughters will cease to be Greek, will rightly assimilate the nationality of their husbands and be lost to us. Attitudes are changing, but we still need more time before we feel comfortable with all the customs of our European partners.'

'And your sons?' she challenged, aware, as she had been all evening, that Alexos's gaze had hardly ever left her. 'Do you feel possessive of them?'

'A different matter entirely!' Theo answered gruffly. 'The foreign women our sons marry bring fresh blood to our strain, but they bear Greek children and that is what matters. This country has had a long and turbulent history and it has stood firm against a host of invaders, so we have a strong sense of national identity.'

'You surely don't doubt the genuineness of my father's hospitality?' Alexos enquired sweetly, his thigh pressing warmly against hers as he moved to place one arm along the back of the couch, his hand turning to brush her cheek before she felt, to her horror, his fingers playfully touch the lobe of her ear as he continued reasonably, 'Since he was prepared to see his own blood diluted by a foreign strain in his first-born child, he could hardly object to that child following his example, could he?'

Theo's eyes sparked as he rose to the challenge. 'It's always been my dearest wish that Alexandros should find a partner worthy of his steel. Character, not nationality, being the vital ingredient of marital harmony.'

He paused briefly, fixing his hard stare on his eldest son. 'These last few years I prayed that Alexos would discover a woman whose temperament would complement his own, someone whose grace and beauty would find an apt setting in Belvedere in years to come and whose compassion would give her the necessary insight to understand and exculpate him...'

'Pateras!' Alexos was on his feet, his face strangely pale in the subdued light of the blind-shaded room. 'Is all this really necessary?'

'Why not?' Theo regarded his son sombrely. 'Ilona wished to be reassured that she is welcome here as your future wife. I am merely providing that affirmation. Since it disquiets you, then by all means let us change the subject. Had you made any plans for this afternoon?'

'As a matter of fact, I thought I'd stroll across to the boatyard and look over the order book. From what Aristide said to me, the business is doing quite well, despite the general recession.' He rose lazily to his full height to stand looking down at Ilona: a buccaneer disguised as a man of virtue and good intent.

'Do you fancy a walk *agape mou*?' he asked softly, extending his hand to help her rise as if her answer was a foregone conclusion. And if they were truly engaged to be married, wouldn't she rather spend the rest of the day alone with him than anywhere else?

She allowed him to grasp her palm, masking a shiver of anticipation as she felt the hard power of his hand against her own, experiencing an unexpected and embarrassing quiver of excitement as her breasts tautened against the soft aubergine cotton of her dress.

'It's not a great distance.' His speculative gaze lingered on her as they reached the emptiness of the spacious hall. 'And you looked as though you needed rescuing from further cross-examination. Like most of my fellow countrymen, my family have curious and enquiring minds, particularly where prospective marriage partners are concerned.'

'I still feel terrible about deceiving them,' she confessed, keeping her voice low as he led her out into the heat of the mid-afternoon.

'The remedy's in your own hands, *mahtia mou*.' He dismissed her qualms with a light shrug of his shoulders and linking his fingers through hers before she had the presence of mind to withdraw her hand. 'My offer of marriage is still open. You only have to assert your prerogative—change your mind.'

She didn't answer, and from his own silence she assumed he hadn't expected her to.

Leaving the grounds of Belvedere, they walked across country without speaking. Strangely Ilona didn't find the lack of conversation oppressive, as she allowed her heightened senses full reign, enjoying the warmth of the sun on her exposed skin, the brush of the long bleached grass against her legs, the scent of the undergrowth as her sandals crushed the indigenous herbs beneath her feet.

She feasted her eyes on the surrounding flora, which was becoming as familiar to her as that of her native England: giant purple thistles, the tiny yellow stars of wild daisies, the sere stems of drought-dead plants covered in tiny snails. Her ears accommodated the slight soughing of the breeze, mixed with the incessant chirrup of cicadas and the sound of her own progress as she walked across the sun-parched earth, just as her taste-buds acknowledged the sweet spiciness of the scented air as it passed across her tongue. She'd loved the landscape at first sight, but since Alexos had entered her life it seemed to possess a new enchantment.

As they approached the site of the boatyard she was delighted it hadn't despoiled the countryside as she'd half feared. As it was located in a natural cleft within the cliffs, both its lay-out and its air of tidiness fitted in naturally with its surroundings.

Leaving Alexos, at his suggestion, to make his way to the low building that housed the office, she wandered around, admiring the sleek hulls that were in preparation, exchanging friendly greetings with the few craftsmen working there.

'*Thespinis*! May I be one of the first to wish you every future happiness!' At the sound of Aristide's deep voice, Ilona spun round, taking his extended hand and smiling her thanks in the manner expected of her.

'Alexos told you, then,' she commented quietly.

'The whole island knows.' Aristide confirmed her worst fears. 'It's not a thing you could hide in a place like this, although I understand why you kept your secret until Alexos had been welcomed back to Belvedere.'

His dark eyes, bright in his weatherbeaten face, assessed her thoroughly. 'I thank God he is rebuilding his life. Three years is a long time for a man to lose from his youth, especially for an act of chivalry.'

'A what?' Surely she must have misheard him, as a strange dryness invaded mouth and throat?

'Going to the aid of a woman who was being molested by a drunken fool.' He frowned. 'I suppose he would have told you the whole story.'

'A woman? There was a woman involved?' Ilona's heart seemed to plummet to her midriff. 'Who was she?'

'No one knows.' Aristide cast her a sly smile. 'There was no need for her to reveal her identity because the first incident happened in a taverna. The fight came later, much later, in the pine-woods. But that's how it all started—a drunken foreigner annoying a Greek girl.' He lifted his arm to face-level, palm open, elbow bent, and rotated his hand anti-clockwise, middle and forefinger extended upwards as if stirring up a whirlpool in the air. '*Po*, *po*, *po*!' The gesture was typically Greek and one Sophia had used on occasions to indicate something of monumental proportions. 'No one who knew Alexos would expect him to stand by and let that happen. It was a tragedy. The man must have had a thin skull, and Alexos is a strong man, who paid a dreadful penalty for that strength.'

No, he was wrong. Silently Ilona rejected Aristide's verdict. Alexos had been punished not because of his strength but for his lack of control in using it. A tremor of fear trembled beneath her skin, but allied to it was another feeling—disbelief. The Alexos she knew was capable of harnessing his emotions: not subjugating them entirely but keeping them within acceptable bounds. He was mentally and physically powerful enough to keep that power in check...unless... An explanation was forming in her mind, vague pictures...a woman: Alexos protecting a woman, not just any Greek woman, but one he loved enough to avenge to the death. Death! Not his in this case but the man who had insulted her. And whoever she was she hadn't even bothered to put in an appearance at his trial! She had deserted him at his hour of greatest need. Rejected him . . .

A piece of stone crunched beneath Aristide's foot, reclaiming her attention.

'You don't blame him, do you?' she asked slowly.

Her frank stare was returned. 'I don't judge him. No one who knew him well will speak against him. Like yourself, *thespinis*, we see beneath the oak veneer to a heart of a softer wood. Whatever the whole truth of the matter, we will only ever know what Alexos wishes us to know. For us, it is enough that he has come home and, better still, that he has brought his future bride with him.'

'Thank you.' Ilona blinked away a sudden dampness that was blurring her vision. How fortunate was the imperious Greek who had shattered the even tenor of her life to have inspired such goodwill despite the facts. She bit her lip. What facts? Clearly Aristide felt there was much more to the tragedy than had ever been told. Who was the woman he had protected? Was she correct in assuming it must have been someone he loved dearly? Where was she now?

Unless Alexos was prepared to answer her questions she would never know. And why should he? Only one woman might lay claim to the right to know the truth— the woman who would be his wife . . . and that wasn't her . . . was it?

CHAPTER EIGHT

IT WAS a long time before Ilona found escape from her troubled thoughts in sleep that night. Too much had happened too soon, she told herself, making her feelings towards Alexos himself such a tangle of emotions that logical processing of them was impossible. Perhaps in a few days she would have rationalised the whole situation. Certainly by then, if Alexos kept his word, she would be able to leave Kaphos and start her life somewhere else, unhampered by his overpowering presence. The prospect should have brought pleasure. Strangely it didn't.

She'd been glad when the evening meal had finished and she'd been able to escape to her bedroom, pleading a tiredness she hadn't had to feign. Although Calliope had played her part as hostess valiantly, there'd been no disguising that the after-effects of the funeral were beginning to take their toll as the initial euphoria caused by her mock engagement to Alexos gave way to an understandable melancholy.

Nikos appeared to be lost in thought for the greater part of the evening, while Frederica's magnificent eyes were puffy and rimmed with fatigue, and both Alexos and his father, their faces dark with the beards of mourning, spoke to each other in polite monosyllables as if the effort to converse was too painful.

However, when sleep eventually claimed her, Ilona slept well, awakening to find fingers of bright sunlight reaching into her room through the half-lowered shutters.

Seven-thirty, she discovered, blinking at her watch through eyes still bemused by dreams she could only half recall. After taking a refreshing shower in the *en-suite* bathroom she picked a boldly patterned gathered-cotton skirt to wear, matching its predominant colour of turquoise with a sleeveless cotton blouse, choosing to half button it and knot the ends at her trim waist, complementing her outfit by slipping her feet into a pair of casual canvas slip-ons whose soft, bouncy soles would nurse her tender feet over the rocky paths.

Leaving her thick blonde hair to find its own shape in a soft bell framing her face, she made her way towards the main living area, deciding she could always walk round the garden if she was too early for breakfast. At the same time as the thought struck her she smelled the welcoming scent of coffee drifting in from the direction of the patio.

'Ah, Ilona, my dear...' It was Calliope who came to welcome her. 'Won't you join me outside for breakfast? I always think this is the best part of the day, before the sun gets too hot and the shadows too black. I expect Theo will join us in a moment.' She ushered Ilona through the glass-bead curtain, which trembled in the early-morning breeze. 'As for Alexos...' She made a small gesture of despair. 'I no longer know the routine he follows. It's such a long time since he graced us with his presence...' The sentence was allowed to drift into nothingness before the older woman's mouth curled into a smile. 'When he was a child he was always the first one down!'

'A man with strong and urgent appetites,' Ilona laughed, then wished she had phrased her reply more delicately, but Calliope's dark eyes gleamed with answering humour, her gaze straying to Ilona's hands.

'I see Christina's ring fits you as if it had been made for you.'

'Yes.' Ilona touched the proud stones. There was no doubt, she and Theo's first wife had possessed similar long-fingered, slim-knuckled hands. She raised troubled eyes to Calliope's pleasant face. 'I hope you don't mind Alexos's father suggesting I should wear it.'

'Of course not, child!' Calliope reassured her softly. 'Even if it had fitted me...' she splayed plump fingers to show how impossible such a thing would be '...it's only right that it should be worn by her son's wife. Poor woman—she gave him so much love for such a short time—it would give her great joy to know that the woman who is going to spend the rest of her life with him wears it in her stead.'

Ilona winced. Calliope was being kind, but her words did nothing to make her feel any better about the situation in which she found herself. Forcing her face into what she hoped was a grateful smile, she accepted a cup of coffee from her hostess, setting it down on a nearby table and helping herself to a soft floury roll, adding butter and black cherry jam to her plate.

'I do hope you realise what you're taking on with my stepson,' Calliope teased, joining her at the table. 'Has your grandmother's upbringing schooled you to be a docile and obedient wife, I wonder? Because I warn you, my Alexandros hasn't the patience or the temperament to be defied with impunity!'

'Shame on you, Calliope!' Alexos stepped on to the patio, defending himself, his mobile face, clean-shaven now, assuming an expression of affront belied by the husky amusement of his voice. 'Ilona knows I'm the most reasonable of men. In fact, she's made a point of defying me since our first meeting and has escaped totally without

punishment!' His smile accosted her with an intimacy
that brought the blood racing to her face as she remembered the frustration she had unwittingly caused him that
night at the El Greco.

As awareness of his potent sexuality flamed inside her
a wild, unbearably pleasurable feeling flowed through
her like a tide of sweetness. For a few seconds they might
have been alone on the patio, an inarticulate protest rising
to her lips as she tried to repulse the effect his dominant
masculinity was having on her.

There was an awkward little silence while he poured
himself a cup of coffee with a lazy nonchalance, before
Calliope pushed her chair back and rose to her feet.

'There are many things I have to do this morning,'
she excused herself. 'Nikos, Frederica and the children
have arranged to spend the day with Frederica's parents,
and I expect Ilona will want to see some more of the
island, so I'll ask Maria to get the two of you a light
lunch any time you wish it.'

'Perhaps there's something I can do to help you?' Ilona
rose eagerly to her feet, none too anxious to find herself
thrust into Alexos's sole company for an unspecified
length of time.

'Yes.' Calliope's dark eyes regarded her with open
amusement. 'You can keep my wayward son at arm's
length from his father! Yesterday's affable meeting was
almost too good to be true. I wouldn't want anything
to spoil it.' She sighed, then added wistfully, 'I've been
dreaming for a long time of having my family together
again under one roof.'

'Then I guarantee neither Ilona nor myself will do
anything to imperil that happy state of affairs, will we,
agape mou?' Dark brows lifted over blue eyes of a
startling innocence.

'Of course not,' she muttered crossly, angered by what she saw as blackmail, only partially ameliorated by the glow of happiness on Calliope's face as she went back into the house.

'You're despicable!' She turned a stony face on her tormentor. 'I don't know how you can encourage your stepmother to live in a fool's paradise when you know that in a few days' time all her dreams will be shattered.'

Broad shoulders shrugged with dismissive casualness. 'Let her enjoy her illusions while they remain. There'll be time enough for tears when you finally walk out on me. In the meantime I have every faith in your playing the part of the devoted sweetheart.' He paused, contemplating her with unnerving stillness. 'Because, however you may feel about the situation, it's quite foreign to your nature to inflict unnecessary pain on the vulnerable.'

Ilona drew her breath in sharply, her feelings running dangerously close to the surface. What was there about this man that played havoc with her reason? What utter arrogance he had to believe he could judge her after such a brief time of being in her company! Yet if that was so, what about herself? Given the task of compiling a thumbnail sketch of his character, she wouldn't be lost for words, would she?

'Among whom I assume you include yourself?' she enquired tartly, to be rewarded by finding herself the subject of a gaze so piercing that she felt as if she'd been pinned to the campsis-covered wall that loomed behind her.

'No, Ilona,' he responded quietly. 'Once, perhaps, a long time ago, but age and experience harden a man, a prison completes the job. If I ever had a tender heart you can be assured that now it is as callused as my hands.' He turned his open palms towards her. Beautiful hands.

A man's hands. That part of his anatomy which made him forever superior to other animals: the thumb at right angles to the palm, giving him the power of grasping, the potential of building and enhancing his environment: the power to create, and with it—the power to destroy...

For one absurd moment she wanted to go forward, take his carelessly displayed hands and hold them to her face. Before she could move, he pre-empted her, abandoning his pose to drain his coffee-cup with a flourish. 'And, now we've determined that my motives are always self-interested and I have no better nature to be appealed to, how about following Calliope's suggestion and letting me show you something more of Kaphos?'

'Why not?' She might as well act out her part as well as possible while it lasted, and it would be less of a strain not to be under the approving smiles of Alexos's family!

'Then I suggest we take a picnic lunch with us and go to one of the beaches. Put a swimsuit beneath your dress and bring a towel and plenty of sunscreen.'

'Yes, sir!' She jumped to her feet, saluting smartly, and felt her heart lurch as her sauciness was rewarded by Alexos's charming grin. At moments like those it was impossible to believe in the dark incident that haunted his life. If only, she thought as she made her way to her room to locate her pretty floral one-piece swimsuit, if only... if only the tourist involved had gone somewhere else for his holiday, if only he hadn't over-indulged... if only the Greek girl involved had stayed at home... Again the girl's identity niggled her mind. Why hadn't Alexos mentioned her existence? Probably, she thought moodily, because, despite the way he was using her to gain his own ends, he wasn't prepared to reveal too much of his inner self to her. She expelled her breath in despair. Was he really as tough as he had averred? Or did his internal scars hide a vulnerability so deep that only the woman he loved would be allowed to know its existence?

Thoughtfully, she slipped into the swimsuit, checking her silhouette in the long mirror provided. Sophia hadn't approved of bikinis, dismissing them as unsubtle as well as unflattering, and Ilona hadn't felt strongly enough about the matter to oppose her, so that both the swimsuits she possessed were one-pieces. Sophia had been no mean judge, she accorded to herself with a half-smile. The multicoloured stretch nylon Lycra with its high-cut legline moulded her body with loving fidelity, supporting and caressing the high, full curves of her creamy breasts, the dipping neckline drawing attention to the youthful cleavage, while the bias cut of the material minimised her already slender waist and caressed the slight womanly curve of her abdomen with gentle control, while the whole of her caramel-coloured back was exposed to the sun's caress, ensuring that she had no ugly strap marks to contend with.

Would Alexos approve? Hastily she thrust the thought away from her. The last thing she needed was Alexos's approval. Like all men, Alexandros Faradaxis possessed a reflex reaction to the female sex. Any woman would do to assuage his male appetite—any *willing* woman, she corrected herself out of a sense of fairness. Swiftly she searched for her bottle of sunscreen, applying a thin film to her face and body before bundling the bottle into her beach bag together with a towel and a few tissues, before stepping inside her skirt and buttoning her blouse.

That night in the El Greco Alexos had wanted a woman—a female body to possess and dominate, warm arms and a soft body to help him forget his sins—and what sins! Like some character from a Greek tragedy, she'd been there, and the Fates had pushed her centre stage...

She'd always thought that when she fell in love with a man it would be someone she could respect. A man of honour, who in his turn loved and respected her. Someone who saw her as an individual, who wanted her for herself, not just because she had the right number of chromosomes. She wouldn't be tricked by good looks or charismatic bearing; nor allow her own sexual needs to be awakened by a man who was not worthy of the love and devotion she knew she could give to someone who really loved her as much as she loved him.

And look what had happened! Her bones had melted and her blood rushed through her veins whenever she'd come into close contact with Alexandros Faradaxis.

He was waiting for her as she came down the few steps from her room, his own towel slung over one shoulder, a small hamper by his side. Instead of the light grey casual trousers he'd worn to breakfast, his long, firmly muscled legs were now displayed in brief belted tan shorts, which matched the contrasting shoulder strip of his pale cream cotton-knit shirt.

'How far away is this beach?' she asked as they left the house and turned away from the village.

'About half an hour's walk.' He shot her a quick appraising look. 'Not too far for you, is it?'

'Of course not.' She fell into step beside him, aware that he adjusted his long stride to match her shorter measure.

After a while, entering the cool beauty of a pine-wood, she felt the tension of her calf muscles lessen as their path took a downward turn. Savouring the pungent scent of the fresh pine, she began to relax. This country was in her blood, welcoming her like a lost child. The feeling

of destiny fulfilled was so strong at that moment that,
despite the warmth of the day, she couldn't repress the
shiver that edged its way down her spine.

'You're cold?' Alexos shot her a look of concern as
his quick glance perceived her movement. 'Not long
now—you can see the ocean!'

He was right. Through the maze of trees she caught
the glitter of turquoise water and knew they were within
yards of their destination. Giving way to a mounting
feeling of excitement, she broke into a run.

Breathlessly she pulled up as her sandalled feet left
the dry earth of the wood to sink into a beach com-
prising tiny shells. Totally deserted, it swept in a curve
of whiteness, lapped by a sea of the palest aquamarine
she had ever seen. Before the shoreline gave way to the
pine trees its shape was broken by clumps of low-growing
cacti and the sprawling leaves of sea lilies.

'Well?' Alexos's lengthy stride had brought him to her
side in seconds. 'Was it worth the walk?'

'It would have been worth twice the walk!' She turned
to face him, her own face alive with pleasure. 'I thought
the Mediterranean had long since given up all its secret
beaches to the tourists!'

'Not yet, thank God!' He extended a lazy arm and
slid it around her shoulders, drawing her closer to him.
It was a warm, friendly gesture and one she was in no
mood to repulse, although she did make a definite effort
not to relax against the pulsating warmth emanating from
his body. Like an animal scenting danger, she held her
ground, every fibre of her body tensed to defend herself
against any move that threatened her, as he added, 'Like
a good hotelier, it still reserves some of its best locations
for lovers.'

There was no mistaking the husky note that deepened his voice and sent her senses screaming. But if he was going to tease her then she was prepared to combat him!

'Then I hope we won't be evicted when it discovers that we are merely play-actors!' Quickly she loosed herself from his hold, relieved when he made no effort to restrain her. 'I can't wait to cool off.'

With fingers that trembled she unbuttoned and un-knotted her blouse, slipping it from her shoulders, before running down to the water's edge. Within a yard of it she stepped out of her skirt, kicked off her shoes and waded in, uncomfortably conscious of Alexos's gaze pinned on her every movement.

It was only when she was neck-high in the water that she dared to look back at the beach. He was standing at the water's edge, still fully clothed, and for a moment she thought he had no intention of joining her. She was wrong. Slowly he stretched, muscles tensing then relaxing. Adonis silhouetted against the dark trees of his homeland, Ilona thought poetically, then scolded herself for her romantic whimsy. But he *was* beautiful, in the way that any healthy animal in the prime of its life was beautiful. Just as she'd been drawn to him on the boat, so now she couldn't drag her eyes away from him as he crossed his arms to grasp the lower edges of his shirt and draw the garment up over his head in a lazy action that made his pectorals swell and his lean abdomen hollow between his ribs.

If she had undressed in double-fast time then Alexos was disrobing in double slow! Was he simply enjoying the sensuous sensation of taking his clothes off in the open air? she wondered, glad that he couldn't possibly be aware of the fascination his actions held for her. It was only when, after taking his time in undoing his belt, he began to lower his shorts to reveal dark maroon bathing trunks that she realised how absurdly she was acting. Her face felt abnormally warm, due to the reflection from the water, no doubt, she assessed, determining that the further away from Alexos she kept, the healthier it would be for her.

Allowing her feet to leave bottom, she turned on her stomach and began her slow, schoolgirl breast-stroke, following the shoreline to the far end of the beach. It was only when she waded ashore as the sand gave way to rocks that she appreciated how quickly her heart was beating and realised she'd been expecting Alexos to overtake her at any time. For a heart-wrenching moment she could see no sign of him. As thoughts of cramps pounded her brain, fear rose in her throat, only be be dispersed when after a few moments she was able to pick out a dark head way out to sea, apparently in no difficulties.

Not a strong swimmer herself, she decided to make her way back to the shade of the trees via the beach, stopping now and then to examine a shell or stand of seaweed, or some exquisitely coloured stone washed smooth by the endless passage of the sea. Reaching for her towel, she rubbed herself down, applied sunscreen to all her exposed parts and, choosing a patch of dappled shade, lay down and closed her eyes.

Some time later she became aware of a faint, irritating tickle on her cheekbone and lifted a lazy hand to discover the source. Her fingers closed round a head of grass. Surprised, she opened her eyes, confused to find the other end of it suspended between two of Alexos's fingers.

'How long have you been back here?' she asked, sitting up abruptly and adjusting that halter-neck of her swimsuit.

'About two hours,' came the laconic reply.

'Oh, surely not!' Her watch was in her beach bag and she began to scrabble inside it, her eyebrows rising in astonishment as she found it and realised he hadn't been teasing her. 'Oh good grief! Why didn't you wake me up?'

'Why should I have?' He was sitting beside her, leaning forward, resting his arms on his raised knees, his head turned in her direction, eyes half shuttered against the brightness of the day. 'You obviously needed the sleep and you'd chosen your place well. There was no danger of your tender skin burning; besides, I enjoyed sitting here, watching you.'

There was a wealth of meaning in those words that she didn't want to dwell on. Already she could feel an edginess prickling her nerves at the mere thought of his sombre eyes taking their uncensored toll of her. In its own way it was a violation of her privacy, and one for which she had been principally to blame.

'Because you should have!' she snapped illogically.

'Well, now I have, *agape mou*,' he returned equably. 'And for the best of reasons . . .' He swung his body, still clothed only in bathing trunks, towards her, lifting a gentle hand to brush away a patch of sand adhering to one of her shoulders. 'You see, for the past two hours I've been sitting here debating whether or not I should kiss you, and I've finally decided that I should.'

'Alexos!' She should have been angry, but no matter how hard she tried to simulate annoyance the emotion wouldn't register on her face. Even the way she'd said his name had sounded more like an invitation than a rebuttal, she acknowledged in horrified realisation. Her sleep had left her lethargic, enervated by the warmth and silence of this mini-paradise—there had to be some reason!

Too late she tried to scramble to her feet, but he caught her to him as she began to rise, pulling her unresisting body towards him, sliding his legs forward and holding her so that with a little gasp she landed on top of him on the warm sand.

'You can't say you weren't warned,' he mumbled, his face buried in her hair, as his arms enfolded her.

This was the time to struggle. Instinct told her that if she put up a fight he would release her. Instead she hesitated, wondering at how comfortable his body was to lie on: firm and supple, yet excitingly solid. By then it was too late, and as his mouth sought hers she responded to his growing desire, opening her lips to welcome his ravishment, thrilling as she heard his harshly indrawn breath as he gloried in her compliance . . . 'to kiss the sugar . . .'

Too late she became aware that his agile fingers had reached behind her neck to undo the catch of her halterneck. Her face flamed. How could she have been so stupid to fall into this trap so soon after all her good resolutions?

'Alexos, no—you mustn't!' she beseeched as he smoothed the material away from her upper body with a small sigh of pleasure, his hands cool on her heated flesh.

'I must, *agape mou*, I must.' Gently he defied her.

Using all her strength in an attempt to break his hold, she strained away from his encroaching mouth, afraid of herself: afraid of the passions he could ignite within her.

For a moment he paused, his face serious, his eyes softly dark behind their veil of heavy lashes, his breath warm and sweet on her flesh. 'Give yourself to me,' he murmured huskily, 'let me make love to you. I want you so much.'

She ought to cry 'No!' But it would be misleading because already her breasts, free of the confining swimsuit, were reacting in their own way to the growing sexual tension, swelling and hardening beyond her conscious power to control. With shocked acceptance of her own desire she knew she wanted Alexos to pay them tribute, to honour them with his own body... 'To open paradise...'

'Yes,' he said with a sigh, half-triumph, half-relief, voicing the word she dared not utter. Gently he lowered her away from his chest so his hands could cup her pendant breasts, offering them to his mouth, his breath quickening, his eyes narrowed to slits yet disturbingly, glisteningly aware of the hardening thrust of the dusky tips between his lips.

Incredibly disturbed by what was happening between them, Ilona felt her whole body vibrate with nameless waves of sensation. Undermining her already weakened mental resistance, they aroused an aching emptiness she'd never experienced before.

Entranced by the delicate caresses of Alexos's soft mouth as it cajoled the ripe buds of her breasts to a proud tumescence, she wanted to hold his dark head to herself, encourage him to suckle her sweetness. Impulsively she ran her fingers through the wealth of ebony hair as her back arced in ecstasy. Oh, dear lord, how she wanted above everything to compensate with her own body for the dreadful days he'd spent shut away from the world and all its pleasures most people took for granted . . . to let him 'possess the lily.'

Scarcely aware of what she was doing, she gasped out his name, time and again, the syllables tremblingly poised between pleasure and protest. It was only when, her whole body pitched to a peak of receptivity, she became shockingly aware of the level of arousal Alexos's beautiful male body had reached that she panicked, shrinking from the blatant evidence of his virile masculinity with a cry compounded of apprehension and dissent.

Alexos expelled his breath in a long-drawn-out sigh of resignation as he sensed her withdrawal. Then he was replacing the soft fabric of her costume to hide her pale flesh, easing her body from his own so he could fasten the clasp at the back of her neck. Raising himself on one elbow, grimacing wryly at his own discomfort, not attempting to hide the frustration that shuddered through his lean frame, he stared at her with passion-darkened eyes.

'Tell me, was this Englishman—this Philip whom you mourn—was he your lover?'

Oh, dear heaven! Wasn't it bad enough he'd made her feel like this—physically limp and boneless, mentally and emotionally confused? How could she be expected to talk about her past when she was caught up in the thrall of the vital sexual force he was exerting to overwhelm her?

'That's my business!' she answered him sharply, her fingers rising in agitation to test the security of the clasp at the back of her neck and finding it perfectly placed.

'Was he your lover?' For all the attention he'd given her answer, she might as well have kept silent.

'No!' She was still trying to steady her breath. 'Although you have no right to——'

'Why not?' He transfixed her with his deep blue gaze, his voice little more than a growl. 'Why not, Ilona? You were planning to be married...he must have wanted you. Why didn't you let him make love to you?'

'Because...' She paused, frowning, wanting to deny her scowling companion an answer yet driven to answer him by the compelling force emanating from him. '...Because my grandmother was Greek!' she returned angrily at last. 'Not metropolitan Greek, but island Greek! I was brought up to believe in the doctrine of pre-marital virginity! Surely you of all people can understand that?'

It was only a half-truth: her conditioning had been reinforced by her own inclination. She'd felt no sense of sacrifice in adhering to Sophia's principles. In retrospect, she was glad! If she and Philip had been lovers how more humiliating it would have been when he'd fallen in love with someone else.

'Perhaps.' Alexos's expression was unreadable as he sawed in a deep breath. 'Certainly the doctrine used to exist but how diligently it was followed would be open to question.'

'Clearly you're speaking from experience!' she retorted fiercely.

'You could say that.'

'Oh!' Warm colour swept into her cheeks as she remembered the girl to whom he'd been betrothed and who had found another man in his absence. Then she lifted her chin firmly, confronting him. 'Surely, then, you don't despise me for having principles?' she asked shakily, unbearably conscious of the threatening beauty of his ardent body, the anguished poignancy of his dark face.

Confronted by such militant masculinity, her own body began to mutate and liquefy. In that moment she was entirely at his mercy with no way to hide it.

CHAPTER NINE

IT WAS a battle to prevent her mouth from trembling as her eyes stung with repressed tears. Ashamed of the way she'd accepted and encouraged his passionate caresses, Ilona turned her head away.

'Ilona...' Alexos stooped slightly, reaching for her, lifting her effortlessly to her feet. She tried to keep her gaze averted but he was having none of it. Gently but firmly he turned her chin, forcing her to look at him, his heavy-lidded eyes sliding over her embracingly.

'Don't be angry with me; I believe you, and I admire your principles, but it wasn't the answer I wanted.' He paused reflectively, seeing nothing but puzzlement on her face. 'I wanted to hear you say that he'd never been your lover because you didn't love him enough to give yourself to him!'

'That too...' He'd forced the truth from her. 'I thought at the time that I did,' she admitted bravely. 'My grandmother approved of him, you see. He was good-looking and polite, and we liked the same kind of food and music and literature...'

'But he didn't turn your blood to fire or fill your dreams?'

'He was sensible and efficient! I don't know how I would have coped if he hadn't been beside me to help me through the arrangements after Sophia's death!'

'So you liked him and depended on him when you were grieving,' Alexos summed up grimly. 'But he couldn't make you want him, the way I can make you

139

want me, hmm?' His dark eyes took an impertinent toll of her body, caressing it as effectively as his husky voice caressed her ears.

She would have denied it if there'd been the smallest chance he would have believed her, but her wanton body had already betrayed her.

'You're an expert,' she accused, a tinge of bitterness colouring her soft voice. 'And I was an easy prey from the first, but I'm not going to forsake my principles just because you...I...you...' she stumbled miserably, unable to voice her feelings.

'Because I can make you feel like a desirable woman instead of a comfortable companion to take to a concert or dine out with?'

She winced at his sarcasm even as his hands reached for her shoulders. 'But you already know there's no need for you to sacrifice your principles to enjoy the pleasures of the flesh.' His thumbs moved slowly on her soft skin. 'And, believe me, I'd do my utmost to make your introduction to them an experience we should both remember for the rest of our lives. All you have to do to salve your conscience and indulge your body is to make this temporary arrangement permanent!' His fingers tightened on her bare flesh as his voice softened and intensified. 'Be my wife, Ilona! Already you wear my mother's ring. All you have to do is honour its intention.'

Her throat parched, her mouth still flavoured with his kisses, her breasts pulsating from his ardent caresses, Ilona searched his fervid face. 'We hardly know each other...' But, entranced by the purpose mirrored in his indigo eyes, she knew she hadn't spurned the idea completely, although every instinct warned her against succumbing to his powerful spell.

'Then we can spend the rest of our lives discovering each other.' He dismissed her protest with casual contempt. 'In my experience, all principles have a price, and I'm prepared to pay yours. What more do you want? Do you think I'm not able to provide a comfortable lifestyle for you? Would you like a full statement of my assets?'

He didn't wait for her answer, continuing ruthlessly, 'I'm not a rich man, but neither am I poor. Eight years ago when I was twenty-five I inherited ten per cent of the shares in Faradaxis Construction, the dividends were invested on my behalf and are now a substantial amount: and then there's the boatyard.' He paused, then added quietly, 'Under my godfather's will I inherit his entire holding, and I can assure you, from yesterday's quick look at the order book, that it's going from strength to strength, added to which——'

'Stop it! Stop it!' Anger at his insistence on her inherent venality sharpened her voice as her brown eyes sparked. 'I'm not interested in your income.'

He smiled without humour. 'Even though it will be sufficient to enable you to buy your clothes in Athens, return to England regularly for a holiday, visit exotic places around the world if you wish to broaden you mind? Even though it means you need never work another day in your life if you prefer not to, or alternatively, should you wish to pursue a business interest, that that too may be possible?'

Wearily she shook her head. How could he so cruelly dismiss any finer feelings she might have? 'Money can't compensate for other things.'

'Like a prison record, you mean?' he asked bitterly. 'Would you find it impossible to hold your lovely head high before the sneers of your contemporaries?'

'No!'

'Is it me you are afraid of, then?' he continued ruthlessly. 'Terrified in case you become a victim of my violence. Is that it, Ilona?'

'No, it's not that, Alexos, I swear it.' The agony mirrored on his face appalled her, and she rushed to reassure him, impulsively lifting her hand to touch his smooth cheek.

Even without Aristide's recent testament to his character still a vibrant presence in her mind, a deep instinct told her that whatever the provocation he would never physically abuse a woman. 'Oh, don't you understand? We have nothing in common.'

'We share a mutual need,' he brushed aside her qualms. 'For a home and family of our own. For nearly six years I've tried to envisage the kind of woman who would be prepared to tie herself to a man with a past like mine. Then I met you and immediately I was drawn to your warmth and beauty...'

'You thought I was a *putana*!' Resentment tore through her. 'You assumed I was available for a price!' The words choked in her throat. Nothing had changed. He still did.

'No, *agape mou*.' His mouth curved into a wry smile. 'I admit I handled the situation badly. My godfather had died very suddenly, doubtless as he would have wished to, but the shock to those who cared for him was great. I was seeking consolation to come to terms with my grief when you appeared like an answer to a prayer.' As his brilliant, intense eyes continued to mesmerise her he slid one hand into her hair, forcing her face to within inches of his own. Was it her own blood's drumming in her ears as her pulse increased its rate that made his voice sound slurred? Or was his powerful body less under his control than she had imagined? She made a feeble effort to draw away, frightened as much by her own reactions as by his fierceness.

'Alexos...' She whispered his name, her voice a thread of sound that scarcely reached his ears.

'Who was I to reject so bountiful a gift from the gods, hmm?' His mouth touched the tip of her nose, drifted to her mouth, brushed her lips. 'I wanted to anaesthetise my pain in the soft anodyne of your body, it is true. I wanted you so badly that in my aberrant state I deluded myself temporarily that you were willing. It was an error of judgement. One I should never have made if my senses hadn't been already so dulled by grief. As soon as I realised my error I left.'

'You're impossible!' She found her voice at last. 'All you want is a woman, any woman who will ensure your acceptance at Belvedere. You're afraid that when I go you'll be forced to leave as well...'

But already the veils she'd drawn across her own emotions were dissolving beneath the barrage of his persistence. Alexos had never pretended that he loved her as she ached to be loved, but wasn't it said that love begot love, so wasn't it possible that in time if she agreed to his proposition she could build on their undoubted physical compatibility to make their union into something worthwhile?

'No,' he corrected her softly. 'Once that might have been true, but no longer. Now it is only you I want as a wife: and as for my being impossible...' He laughed softly. 'Difficult at times, I admit, but never impossible.' The colour of his eyes darkened to Prussian blue as hysterical laughter bubbled in her throat. Everything. He was offering her everything—except the only thing she wanted from him: a declaration that the desire he felt for her was founded in some degree of affection. 'You make it sound as if I'm a candidate at a job interview,' she protested, praying that he would discern the sparkle in her eyes as amusement rather than incipient tears.

He didn't deny it. 'It could be a most rewarding position for the right applicant,' he agreed. 'But I can't lie to you, Ilona. I will try to live down my past—but I can never bury it. The record will always be there for those who wish to cite it, but you'll find that financial success lends respectability to a multitude of sins, and most people have short memories. Besides, there are those charitable enough to say to themselves, ''There, but for the grace of God, go I.'''

He was right, she knew that. People like Aristide, and the family he thought would refuse to accept him into their midst; other nationals of his proud homeland who had blood on their hands because they too had had the courage to protect the weak from unsolicited aggression.

'It's not as simple as that...' Ilona made an effort to control the incipient tremble in her voice as caution and instinct warred within her. Her feelings for Alexos were complex, but wasn't that what love was all about? One thing above all she knew with an astonishing clarity: she wanted to be possessed by him, and she wanted to comfort him when he was unhappy, support him when he was attacked, weep with him when he was sad, laugh with him when he was happy, bear his children with joy... yet to agree to what was virtually a marriage of convenience as far as he was concerned... Could any good come out of it?

'No? Then let me try and make it simpler...'

Gasping as she found herself once more encompassed by his arms, her mouth subjected to a deeply passionate kiss, Ilona felt the last shreds of her reservations draining from her. Instinctively her hands rose to his shoulders before stretching to clasp around his neck as he drew her intimately against the length of his aroused body, naked save for the brief swimming trunks.

She tried to speak, but the words stuck in her dry throat, so she could only stand there while the breeze stirred the pine needles and the cicadas chorused their endless chant as his fingers threaded through her hair, restraining the movement of her head while he pleasured her mouth with the persuasive incursion of his tongue.

She was breathing heavily, her heart thudding with the agitation of a trapped bird, by the time he released her lips, to trail his wanton caresses across her cheekbones and down the soft expanse of her neck. Breathing in the scent of his hair and skin, a warm sensual languor spreading slowly through every limb as her senses swam beneath the touch of his hands and his mouth, she knew she was lost.

Alexos might not love her as she ached to be loved but he desired her, his strong male body trembling with the effort of controlling his natural reactions to her mindless response. It was a start. With no other rival for his love, it would guarantee her the pole position in his life. If it was all he could offer her then if would have to be enough. She would make it enough! Yet once more the spectre of the girl he had risked his reputation and freedom for rose to haunt her. Had she been a stranger? Or had their relationship been much closer? Had the degree of force he'd reputedly used had its roots in the passionate jealousy of a man in love?

'Be honest with me, Ilona.' His breath was warm against her ear. 'You don't want to leave Kaphos. You want to stay here, become my lover...my wife...' His hands moved with deadly purpose down the length of her body, predatory fingers following the soft curves of her waist and buttocks as he gathered her to him in a blatant intimacy.

Her decision made, though still untold, her senses swimming, she ceded to her own needs, running her palms down the damp, silky skin of his naked back, daring to trace the hard hollows of his loins, experiencing a fierce surge of desire as he bucked beneath her touch as if she had sent several volts of electricity through his flesh.

He was right. She didn't want to leave him. Not because of his bribes and promises, but because she loved him with every melting cell of her body and brain... and heart.

'Admit it.' His voice was hoarse, his eyes narrowed and searingly powerful as his fingers tangled once more in her hair to hold her head so that she couldn't turn it away from his impassioned scrutiny. 'Tell me you'll marry me...'

She was already vanquished. Quickly she lowered her eyelids, afraid that his penetrating gaze should discover the full extent of her vulnerability.

'Yes,' she whispered, the word escaping from her throat as a husky sob. 'Yes, Alexos, if you're sure that's what you really want, then I will marry you.'

She had no idea how long it was before he broke the embrace that followed her capitulation, or any detailed memory of what pleasures they had exchanged, just a deep, languid feeling of bliss as their mouths met and parted and met again and their hands roamed at will, loving, discovering, exciting...

'Not yet, not here...' It was Alexos who broke the lethargic, sensual magic enthralling her, speaking with an effort, his voice husky and shaky, as he gently released her. 'I need time and privacy to make love to you as you deserve to be loved.' His eyes appeared black as he looked at her, the pupils distended. 'We must try to reach your father, write to him, phone him, whichever is easier.' He gave her a sharp look. 'You do have his address?'

She nodded. Michael Frankard was, after all, her next of kin. 'But I'm twenty-two. I don't need his consent,' she protested.

'But it would be right to have his blessing, *ne*?'

'Yes. Yes, it would.' Perhaps it was because of the family closeness she'd witnessed at Belvedere that the idea of contacting her father and his new family seemed suddenly attractive. She sighed, recognising the truth. It wasn't that her father hadn't loved her. Only that he had loved her mother more.

'Good.' Alexos's eyes were bright with the glow of success. 'We'll have our picnic and then we'll find the priest. You've already agreed that July the twentieth will be a good date for our wedding?'

She had, but of course at the time it had been a meaningless pleasantry. Now it was going to be for real.

For a few seconds she stood motionless, her breathing shallow as her dark eyes swept over the form of the man she loved, absorbing the glossy darkness of his hair, the strong bones of his face, assimilating the physical beauty of his tough male body, while her heart beat with the intense concentration of a drum solo. In time perhaps he would confide in her about the events that had led to his disgrace, because, like Aristide, she sensed he had been more sinned against than sinning. But for now because she loved him she would have to trust him. Trust him with the remainder of her life.

She drew in a deep breath to steady her nerves. 'The twentieth will be fine,' she agreed in a firm voice.

Dinner had been served at eight-thirty, and a surreptitious glance at her watch confirmed that the time was fast approaching eleven as she accepted a *mantarini* liqueur to accompany her coffee.

Conscious of Alexos's eyes resting on her across the table, she offered him a contented smile.

'Happy?' he asked softly, lowering his voice so that it passed unnoticed beneath the buzz of general conversation.

'Very,' she returned laconically, matching his tone.

'No regrets?' His dark brows rose interrogatively.

'None,' she returned, believing it. 'None at all!'

It was gone midnight when the small party broke up, although the children had left the table at nine, after having had their own meal with the adults.

Alexos was still talking to his half-brother and sister-in-law when she left the dining-room. Tired and a little flushed from the unusual amount of alcohol she'd consumed during the evening, she offered him her cheek as she wished him *kali nicta*. Solemnly he brushed his warm mouth against her cheekbone and she drew in her breath, catching the scent of warm male flesh enhanced by the hint of a natural erotic muskiness.

Conscious of the two other people in the room, she restrained the urge to fling herself into his arms and offer him her mouth as he murmured, '*Kalon ipno, agape mou.*'

Would he come to her room? He'd shown no reluctance to do so that first night they'd met—and with less encouragement! She smiled to herself. And this afternoon—if Nikos and his family hadn't arrived back unexpectedly early because Frederica's mother had developed a migraine, wouldn't she and Alexos have become lovers? Every cell of her aroused body clamoured for him. It had been a kind of agony, sitting so near to him all evening, yet deliberately playing her feelings down so as not to embarrass his family.

The interview with the priest had been interesting and rewarding. As they had sat in the best room of his small house beside the Byzantine-styled Greek Orthodox church that dominated the square at the back of the small town, sipping thick black Greek coffee, it had soon become apparent that the priest's attitude towards Alexos was one of friendliness—even affection. On such a small island weddings were comparatively rare, and there would be no problem with the date they'd selected once the relevant papers had been provided.

All that had remained was to contact her father in the States, and this she'd attempted to do immediately on her return to Belvedere by telephone. Unfortunately he'd been away on business but she had exchanged a pleasant few moments of conversation with her stepmother and had been assured that her father would get in touch with her as soon as possible, and that there was no doubt he would not only be delighted for her but also eager to attend the ceremony.

Freed from her confining garments, she stretched luxuriously before pulling her cotton nightdress over her head. If Alexos did come she wouldn't turn him away. This new kind of love she'd discovered, she reflected ruefully, was powerful enough to disarm the conditionings of a lifetime.

Her nerves on edge, she restlessly paced the room. How could she sleep with her senses so enlivened? With a small sigh of impatience she turned out the light before opening the balcony door and stepping out into the warm night air. A few moments for her pupils to adjust and she was aware of the multitude of stars in the sky, able to make out the outline of the fountain and various shrubs.

Seating herself so that she could rest her arms on the balcony wall, she amused herself by trying to identify some of the other garden features. It was then she became aware of a movement—a flash of light-coloured material against the dark bushes. Alexos? Her heart seemed to miss a beat as she recognised the silver-grey trousers and pale blue shirt he'd worn at dinner. Couldn't he sleep either? Like hers, was the adrenalin flowing too richly through his blood as he made the effort to respect Sophia's upbringing?

A thrill of anticipation made her shiver. She would lean over the balcony like Juliet welcoming her Romeo, and everyone who knew their Shakespeare knew how that had ended! On the point of doing so, she hesitated as another figure came into view from the direction of the house.

'Frederica!'

She tensed with shock as Alexos's low-pitched voice, sharp with emotion, broke the silence of the night and he moved towards his sister-in-law's form, coming to a halt only a few yards away from where she sat, invisible in the deep shade of the balcony.

'Alexos—oh, Alexos *mou*.' As Ilona froze into immobility the Greek girl flung her arms open wide, drawing Alexos into their warmth, pulling his dark head down on her shoulder.

A surge of bitter, painful jealousy seared Ilona's heart. By any standards their greeting was far more affectionate than their relationship merited. She felt sick as

in instant recall other pictures flashed across her mind—
Frederica's face when she had seen Alexos for the first
time, Nikos's early reticence in his brother's presence,
the unspoken tension of the previous evening...the
loaded looks that she'd intercepted more than once
passing between the two half-brothers at dinner a few
hours ago...

Sensing the heaviness of the emotional atmosphere,
she was too dazed to analyse it, her fingers clutching at
the balcony rail for support. She should return to her
bedroom and close the blinds, but doing so might draw
attention to herself. It was an added humiliation she
couldn't risk.

It was Frederica who broke the embrace, pushing
Alexos away from her to gaze up into his eyes, an expression of naked love reflected on her classic features
highlighted by the moonlight, the message of adoration
so painfully clear on her beautiful face that Ilona's mouth
went dry at the sight of it.

'I saw you out here in the garden and I knew I had
to speak to you, but now we're alone together I don't
know what to say to you, my dear.' Nikos's wife spoke
softly, but her clear voice carried audibly in the still night
air, a hint of tears plainly discernible in its intonation
as her hand was raised to stroke Alexos's face in an intimate gesture of love. 'You sacrificed so much for me...I
still have nightmares about that dreadful man, the way
he grabbed me. I can't regret what happened to him,
only that you paid the price for it! I know we swore we'd
never mention it again...'

'Then don't,' his deep voice chided her, but it was
tinged with amusement rather than annoyance as he lifted
a lean hand to caress the top of her sleek head. 'Just tell
me how glad you are about my plans.'

'Glad! I'm overjoyed!' Her reply, heavy with unshed tears, reached Ilona's ears easily as she remained transfixed, just above their field of vision, her heart beating like a sledge-hammer. 'Oh, my dear, there's so much I want to say to you—my heart is so full...' She paused, then continued, her voice unsteady, 'You know how I feel about you: how I'll never forget what happened...' Her voice broke.

'Hush, Frederica.' It was little more than a murmur of consolation but it pierced Ilona's heart with the pain of a well-thrown dart. 'It's over now. We all have to forget it.'

'But I feel so ashamed about the way I treated you. We were still betrothed, everyone expected we would marry...'

'An outdated custom that no one takes seriously.' He dismissed her scruples lightly. 'You only acted as any girl in your position would have done.'

'Perhaps...' She sounded doubtful, but her voice lightened as she continued softly, 'Well, what I really came out here to tell you is that for every moment of joy and love you've given me, I wish you ten!'

It was more than Ilona could bear! As a sudden surge of wind caught the windchimes and sent them tinkling, momentarily distracting the two figures in the garden, she seized the opportunity to slink back into her room.

Somehow in the darkness she found her way to her bed, collapsing on to it as her legs seemed to jellify.

She'd been right all along. There had been—still was—something special between Alexos and his beautiful sister-in-law. What she'd just overheard proved it beyond doubt. Frederica was the girl to whom he'd been betrothed. It was she who had been the cause of the tragic fight that had resulted in Alexos's going to gaol. She and Alexos had been lovers too—what other way was there to interpret the moments 'of joy and love' Alexos had given her? Yet, as soon as Alexos's back had been turned, she had married his half-brother.

Why? Outrage on Alexos's behalf temporarily blinded Ilona to her own misery. Had Frederica been unable to face up to his disgrace, panicked when he'd been arrested and turned to Nikos for comfort? Little wonder that Alexos had spoken about being resigned to spend the rest of his life alone. How could any woman who purported to love a man desert him so cruelly?

In her anguish Ilona hugged her knees and began to rock backwards and forwards on the bed. If only she'd refused that last liqueur—her brain might be sharper. Somewhere, locked in her subconsious mind, was the answer to this painful enigma, if only she could get her numb brain to work.

Not only had Frederica deserted the man she was betrothed to marry, but she must have also done so remarkably quickly after his arrest, because she and Nikos celebrated their sixth wedding anniversary next month— how bitterly ironic now the suggestion that she and Alexos should share the same date!

Slowly, her misery deepening, the clouds were clearing from Ilona's mind as she pieced together the meagre information she possessed. Alexos had been in prison for three years and had been away from Belvedere for a further two, so that meant Nikos had married Frederica some time after Alexos's arrest and before his trial and commitment.

Unfaithful Frederica! It all fitted. How could she have brought herself to act so hastily—when it was so obvious that she still cared deeply for the man she had spurned? Through the remaining mists in Ilona's mind a powerful word presented itself—*pregnancy*.

But that was absurd, wasn't it? Xeni was only five. But when? Of course! St Polyxena's Day. In a flash she was off the bed, fumbling for the bedside light, filling the room with its soft glow. On the table beside her was her diary: the five-year Greek diary that had been a gift from Sophia. Every day acknowledged a saint. She would start at January and work her way through. Seconds later her moving finger halted at January the twenty-fourth.

It was true, then. If Xeni had been five in the January before the July in which her parents celebrated their sixth wedding anniversary she had been conceived three months before that wedding. So Xeni, who bore so much resemblance to Alexos, could be, almost certainly was, his daughter.

Of course Nikos knew. No man would be simple enough to accept a six-month baby as his own. Even that restrained, diffident greeting between the two men on the patio lent substance to the theory. Nikos, too, must have loved Frederica, because surely he wouldn't have been altruistic enough to marry her just to give his brother's child a name—unless Theo had made it worth his while by giving him his present position in Faradaxis Construction? Theo, who was so anxious to see his heirs inherit Belvedere that he would have moved heaven and earth to keep Alexos's child in the family, in the hopes that it would be a boy.

Ilona shivered spasmodically. How ironic, then, that the child should be a girl and that Frederica, having borne Nikos his own female child later, should become barren. Whatever the reason for Frederica's betrayal, the facts remained the same: not only did Alexos not love her, Ilona, but he was also still deeply enamoured of his sister-in-law. She had just seen and heard the proof with her own eyes and ears.

A sob of anguish escaped her lips as tears fell unheeded from her eyes, trailing down her cheeks to fall unrestrained on the soft cotton of her nightdress. Alexos's motives for his determined siege to her emotions were becoming clearer all the time. Not only was he a virile male with a normal sex drive that craved to be satisfied, but casual sex would never have been enough for him if he wanted to return to Belvedere.

If he was to meet Frederica and Nikos socially, and to enjoy seeing his own daughter reach womanhood, it would be imperative for him to appear happily married to avoid scandal. Nikos might not possess his half-brother's obvious authority, but, from what she had seen of him, Ilona suspected he had enough of the Faradaxis heritage of pride to keep his wife away from any other marauding male.

So Alexos had been correct when he said he would be more welcome at Belvedere if he brought a future bride with him, although his reasons had been far more complex than he'd chosen to admit, and she'd been stupid enough to believe that, whatever disappointments he'd had in the past, she could, with patience and the power of her own love, win his affection.

CHAPTER TEN

DEAR God! What a simple, naïve fool she'd been! Now Ilona could see there was one other reason she'd been ideal for the role in which she'd been cast: despite her vestige of Greek blood, she was a foreigner, who'd been a thousand or so miles away at the time of the original tragedy. Six years ago Alexos's crime would have made headlines in the local papers. Even now his presence attracted unnatural curiosity. How difficult it would have been for him to find a local girl who, knowing the facts, would agree to take on such a thankless task as that of wife to a man whose heart was already possessed by his own brother's wife!

His own brother's wife! The words repeated themselves inside Ilona's brain. Were Alexos's motives even more dishonourable? Did he intend to lull Nikos into a feeling of false security by flaunting her, Ilona, as the love of his life so that beneath the camouflage she provided he could take up once more his amorous relationship with Frederica?

It was the final straw needed to break her self-control. Sobbing bitterly, she flung herself face down on her bed, her fists pummelling the pillow as her tears soaked through its fine cambric cover.

'I hate you, Alexos! I hate you!' She mumbled the words into the soft down, wishing they were true, realising in her agony that it wasn't Alexos she hated . . . only what he had done to her, and what he was proposing to do to the family who loved him.

* * *

It was early the following morning when she dragged herself down to breakfast. On the patio Theo was amusing his grandchildren; in the kitchen Calliope and Maria were discussing menus for the evening meal, while Nikos was stretched out on one of the couches in the living-room, reading a magazine. Of Frederica and Alexos there was no sign.

After exchanging greetings with everyone else she helped herself to coffee, eschewing the spread of rolls and bread, knowing that she would choke if she attempted to eat anything solid.

She'd dressed herself carefully for the dénouement, choosing to wear close-fitting denim jeans and a short-sleeved blouse. Somehow the unisex fashion made her feel less vulnerable to Alexos's undoubted air of masculine authority. This was an occasion on which she not only needed to face him as the equal she was, but also to convince him of that fact, she'd determined grimly.

The scene she anticipated with a curious mixture of apprehension and anger was not going to be one of outraged feminine pique. On the contrary, she was the one who was going to walk out on Alexos! So, in contrast to the neat unisex clothes she'd chosen to wear, she made her face up with great care, using artifice to conceal the ravages of tears and nightmare-ridden sleep.

Frederica arrived a few moments later, looking sleek and beautiful in very short shorts topped with a sleeveless vest-top.

'Nikos and I have promised the children we'll spend the morning on the beach,' she confided to the company as a whole. 'They've been looking forward so much to coming here again that they can't wait to get into the sea.'

'Sounds a good idea.' Alexos strolled on to the patio, hands thrust into the pockets of close-fitting casual trousers in a light shade of grey that matched the short-sleeved cotton-knit shirt stretched across his muscled chest. It was the moment she'd been dreading. Her first sight of him after her awareness of the true extent of his cruel conspiracy.

Her heart lurched and her breath sucked into her throat in sudden tearing pain as he coiled his powerful body into one of the comfortable patio chairs and reached for the coffee jug. 'I have to call in at the boat-yard after breakfast. If you've decided which beach you're going to, Ilona and I might join you later. What do you think, *agape mou*?' An interrogative eyebrow rose in her direction. Instantly she responded to the suggestion of arrogance and authority in his deep-timbred tone.

'Actually I had enough of the beach yesterday.' Shrugging, she dismissed the joy of the experience that had been as false as it had been beautiful at the time, knowing she sounded petulant and not caring. It was all part of the new personality she was about to present to the complacent Greek who had so neatly ripped her heart into pieces.

'In that case we'll find something else to occupy our time.' He smiled easily, his dark-lashed gaze dropping from the challenging expression in her eyes to rest on her provocatively pouting mouth. A faint feeling of unease brought a tremor to her nerves. Infuriated that, despite her contempt for what he'd planned, she could still feel an aching awareness of him, she turned her head away, closing her eyes so tightly that they hurt, effectively blotting out his image.

There was an awkward silence for a few moments before Nikos interposed with a quick laugh. 'A wise decision, Alexos. Time enough to spend building sandcastles and sitting in the shallows when you have your own brood.'

'A prospect I look forward to with eager anticipation,' Alexos responded smoothly, instantly regaining her attention.

As long as you don't expect me to be their mother, she wanted to cry out, every nerve in her body on edge as she restrained herself, equally aware that Theo and Calliope were regarding her with smiling attention, some latent sense of propriety keeping her tongue still.

Unable to control the bitter tightness constricting her throat, she struggled to her feet, murmuring something about looking for her sunglasses, and made her way on shaky legs to the cool sanctuary of the house.

'Ilona—wait! What's the matter? Are you ill?'

She spun round in the passage that led to her room as Alexos's hand fell on her shoulder. His movement to apprehend her had been as fast as a lion striking for the kill.

'I'm fine.' She forced herself to assume a calmness she certainly didn't feel, now that the show-down had been forced upon her. 'It's just that I've had time to think things over and I've decided to go back to Crete.'

'You—what?' The white torment on his face shocked her as he seemed to recoil from her.

Instinctively she too took a step away, increasing the distance between them, glad that he'd detained her before she'd reached her bedroom. Here at least she was within range of help if she needed it, and from the look on his face that wasn't an impossibility.

'I'm sorry—is my Greek that bad?' she asked with carefully assumed lightness. 'What I said was——'

'I know what you said,' he growled, one stride closing the distance she had put between them. 'What I don't understand is what you mean. Why do you want to go back to Crete when we are to be married in a few weeks' time?'

'Oh, that.' Her heart was beating so fast and so painfully that she raised the palm of her hand to her chest in a vain attempt to soothe it.

'Yes, that!' He grabbed her by the upper arms, his hold strong, almost cruel. 'What are you trying to tell me, Ilona?'

'I've changed my mind. I did a lot of thinking last night and I've decided I don't want to marry you after all.' Looking into his lean, angry face, she experienced a sudden spasm of painful desire, a wrenching ache that nauseated her.

'Why?' he demanded harshly, a hard muscle jerking spasmodically beneath his cheekbone, his strong face a taut mask of non-comprehension, his eyes darkly menacing beneath drawn brows. 'What's happened between yesterday and now to make you change your mind?'

Now was her opportunity to spill out the depth of her disillusionment. Her pride forced her to prevaricate. 'Let's just say that I came to my senses. Yesterday on the beach was an aberration. It was a very romantic setting and I fell for its spell. After a night's sleep I came back to reality—that's all there is to it.'

Lines of strain distorted the chiselled lines of Alexos's elegant mouth as his body tensed. 'Look, Ilona, this is ridiculous. We can't stand here like this, discussing our future——'

'We don't have a future—not together.' She swallowed with difficulty as her voice cracked unexpectedly. 'That's what I'm trying to tell you. The subject isn't open for discussion because I've already made my mind up, finally and irrevocably.' She glared at him, loving and hating him in a turmoil of mixed emotion. 'I'm sorry if it means I've ruined your plans, but at least you no longer need me as a reason for staying at Belvedere, do you?'

'That doesn't mean I no longer want you.' His breath rasped in his throat as he stared down into her unresponsive face. 'Or that you don't want me either.' He closed the distance between them, reaching out to grasp her upper arms, his fingers moving convulsively on her soft skin.

There was a hard ball of pain in her chest, but hearts didn't really break, did they?

'Oh, I don't deny that you're a very attractive man, Alexos, and doubtless an accomplished lover, and that for a few moments I was tempted by your offer, especially as you presented such an all-round attractive package.' She forced her mouth into a parody of a smile. 'But that was yesterday. Today I want out.'

'And if I won't let you go?' His voice had a hard, cutting edge that made her skin crawl.

'You can't prevent it!' She fought to quell a small panicky sensation arising in her as his beautiful hard mouth twisted cynically. 'I've got enough money with me to pay Aristide to take me back to Crete, and that's what I intend to do.'

'Only if I allow it!' His dark eyes challenged her decision. 'Since my godfather left me his entire interest in the boatyard, what Aristide does and where he goes depends on me.'

'In that case I'll get the next ferry to one of the nearby islands and try my luck there.' She raised her head to meet his cold gaze with a sparkling challenge of her own.

'You really are determined to leave me, then?' He stared down at her, his expression tautly controlled, his eyes taking a contemptuous toll of her body as she tensed every muscle in an effort to restrict the disconcerting effect they were having on her. 'I must admit that for a while you really had me fooled. I believed...' He paused, choosing not to finish the sentence. 'Is there nothing I can say or do to persuade you to reconsider?'

He sounded as impersonal and detached as she'd ever heard him, his cool tone tearing at her heart. For one unbelievable time-suspended second she wanted to fling her arms around him, renege on her decision and beg him to give her the chance to make him forget Frederica. Mindful of her own weakness, she drew in her breath, knowing that she had to give him a reason he would understand and accept if she was to retain her last few fragments of pride.

'Nothing. The fact is, I've been thinking over what you said and I don't want to get involved with a criminal,' she lied brutally.

'Isn't it a little late for that?' The quiet question unveiled a new note in his voice, warning her that he still hadn't totally accepted her rejection. 'I admit, you were unaware of my background when we first met, but afterwards——'

'Afterwards I reacted to you on a purely physical level. You have a very potent brand of masculinity, as I'm sure you must know.' She stiffened as, apparently encouraged by her words, he let his hands travel to her shoulders. Her legs felt boneless, her breathing constricted at his nearness, but she knew she had to finish what she'd started. 'Physical attraction isn't enough to build a relationship on, Alexos. There has to be respect, and I realise now I could never find that for a man who did what you did.' Quickly she averted her face before he could see the tell-tale tears in her eyes. It was a low blow and one she detested having to deliver, but rather that than have to reveal the sordid truth she'd discovered.

There was a deathly silence, broken only by her own uneven breathing, as Alexos gazed at her, his face a taut mask without expression.

'I see,' he said at last. 'Well, in that case, you're quite right. There's nothing I can do, except have a word with Aristide on your behalf. In the circumstances there seems no point in delaying your departure.'

She'd won, but there was no triumph in it, only a depleting misery that flowed to every cell in her body.

'Thank you,' she whispered. 'I'd better go to my room and get my things together. Do you want me to tell your family that it's all over between us, or would you prefer to wait until I've left Kaphos?'

'Leave it to me,' he instructed brusquely. 'I'll break it to them gently in my own time, and in the circumstances I'll see you're well rewarded financially for the part you've already played.' His mouth twisted cruelly. 'You'll never know how sorry I am that you aren't going to stay around for the final curtain.'

Oh, but she would! Not that she had any intention of telling him so.

'That's not necessary——' She began to refuse his offer of a pay-off, breaking off with a small cry of pain as his fingers dug suddenly into her shoulders and she was pulled hard against him. 'Don't!' she said hoarsely, trying to detach herself with panic-stricken movements.

'I'd appreciate your leaving it to me to decide what's necessary and what isn't.'

His head came between her and the daylight. For a brief space of time she resisted the heated pressure of his mouth; then she was surrendering, the blood storming through her veins, its pressure deafening her. Somehow she managed to raise her hands, sliding them between their two bodies, resting them against his hard chest, feeling the heavy thud of his heart in her palm. Suddenly she'd lost the power of reason. She was dissolving, smouldering, her mouth vanquished under his angry, ferocious demand.

She was trembling when he finally released her, pulling his head back with a long, harsh intake of breath as he glared down at her.

It was all she could do to prevent herself from reeling against the nearby wall as he stepped away from her. Tentatively she raised one hand to her mouth. So that was what was termed a punishing kiss. This was the way Alexos had chosen to demonstrate his frustration at the way she'd ruined his carefully laid plans; and it had been more successful in that purpose than he could ever have imagined, its power trebled, because despite what she'd discovered she wasn't immune to his caresses. She still loved him.

Suddenly she was conscious of the noise from the patio, the rattle of plates and the cries of the children. Life going on as normal at Belvedere. A life she had once believed she might share.

Blindly she turned, brimming tears limiting her vision, to flee headlong to her room. Fumbling at the door-handle, she wondered if Alexos might pursue her further, breathing a sigh of relief once she was inside, leaning against the closed door as she tried to collect her senses together.

Several minutes passed before she could be sure that he'd made no attempt to follow her. Inconvenient as her decision must be for him, at least he had the grace to realise that he was in no moral position to argue his own case further. Listlessly she began to gather her bits and pieces, fitting them into her suitcase. It only took a few minutes but, rather than rejoin the rest of the family, she decided to sit out on her balcony, gazing over the peaceful garden, now deserted. Presumably Nikos had already started out on the journey to the beach with his family, and Calliope and Theo had found other pursuits to occupy them.

Too stunned and unhappy to contemplate the future in any depth, she contented herself by absorbing her surroundings with all of her senses, taking comfort in the touch of the sun, the drone of the cicadas and the light breeze that teased her soft hair.

It was barely an hour later when her introspection was disturbed by a short rap on the door.

'Yes?' She was halfway to opening it when Alexos saved her the trouble, stepping into the room and closing it firmly behind him, to stand surveying her, his mouth tight, his expression guarded.

'Aristide will take you back to Crete this afternoon after lunch.' He smiled tightly. 'You have accommodation reserved and paid for in your name at the El Greco for the next three months, and financial compensation will be waiting for you when you arrive.'

'The El Greco? But...'

Startled, she began to protest, only to have her sentence truncated as Alexos intervened tersely, 'Don't be alarmed, Ilona. I've convinced the manager that your dismissal was a gross error of judgement, and you will be welcomed back there as an honoured guest.' His mouth twisted mockingly. 'Added to which, I can assure you, your accommodation will be a great deal more roomy and pleasant than it was previously!'

'You don't have to do this!'

'Why not? I can afford it and you've earned it.' He dismissed her protest with a casual movement of one hand. 'Even if you are running away before the final curtain.'

Looking into his dark, dangerous face, Ilona felt her stomach muscles tense as she sensed the power of the tamped-down emotion that held him in thrall. Never had she glimpsed such bitterness on anyone's countenance, heard such contempt in anyone's voice. He was hurting badly, and the urge she felt to comfort him was untenable.

'Alexos...don't...' she whispered. 'There will be other women...'

'But not like you, Ilona, with your sugar lips and apple cheeks...'

His voice was husky, throbbing with feeling. Then, before she had the wit to move away, he reached for her, forcing her backwards until her knees buckled and she found herself sitting on the bed with him beside her: arrogant, self-willed, his bruised ego in need of soothing, the male animal uppermost in him at that moment, desire leaping like a flame in his lean and supple body.

When he pushed her backwards with firm but gentle hands she couldn't find the power to resist. When his mouth sought hers with open lips she surrendered to his pain and his passion, allowing its possession, aware of his deep arousal, the tormented pain of his controlled desire, which made his breath ragged as if every tortured gasp would be his last. She knew she should resist for both their sakes, but as his hands sought the buttons of her shirt, slipping them through their tight buttonholes with urgent, clumsy fingers, she trembled, awaiting the feel of his hands on her bare skin with an aching trepidation.

A small sob escaped her as he pushed the soft fabric of her shirt away, dispensing with the clasp of her bra in one brief moment. Even while she despised herself, she gasped her pleasure as the intimacy of his fingers caressed her pale breasts, setting off delicious waves of sensation, causing the apices to swell and harden beneath his marauding touch.

Caught in the spiralling ecstasy he engendered, for one fleeting instant of time she fantasised that he truly loved her, flinging her arms around his eager male body, taking her own pleasure in the strength and tensile beauty of his exquisite musculature, inhaling his intoxicating scent, accepting his weight as he pinned her to the bed, some deep primitive instinct acknowledging and welcoming the power he had to master her. Not just physical power—but the power of a mind and soul that was as complementary to her own psyche as the predatory male body which housed them reciprocated her soft femaleness.

When his mouth homed in on her breasts she thought she would faint, as her whole body clamoured for fulfilment. Clinging to him, aching for appeasement, she could feel his hardness through the light summer trousers he wore, knew he wanted her as much as she craved to take him.

She was still trapped in a spiral of enchantment when he withdrew from her, levering his powerful body away, leaving her caught between hell and heaven, her hair tousled, her clothes in disarray, her senses scattered.

He stood regarding her, every muscle of his face tautly controlled, his eyes dwelling on her exposed flesh with a disdain that made her flinch as hastily she scrabbled to find the clasp of her bra and protect herself beneath its scanty cover of silk and lace.

'So at least you weren't lying about one thing, *agape mou.*' His voice was hard, an accusing edge to it that tore at her heart. 'You still do find my brand of masculinity potent, hmm? Just how far would you have gone, I wonder, if I hadn't called a halt?'

Shame brought a flush to her cheeks as her trembling fingers made heavy work of rebuttoning her shirt. Because she loved him she wouldn't have stopped him. She knew it, but it wasn't anything to which she could admit, if she wished to retain the last few shreds of her credibility.

'If you hadn't changed your mind you would have discovered that for yourself, wouldn't you?' she breathed tightly.

'Yesterday I wouldn't have changed my mind.' Cruelty sharpened the deep blue of his eyes, tightened the line of his hard, beautiful mouth. 'Because yesterday I believed you were going to be my wife.'

Wearily she shook her head, unable to find her voice as her eyes blinked in an effort to hold back unexpected tears.

With a smothered oath he turned away from her, pacing towards the window. 'You can't live with my past—and I can't change it. So, unless you find the prospect of being my lover more acceptable than that of being my wife, the sooner you leave here the better.'

'I'm already packed.' She could tell nothing from the back view he presented to her as she drank in her fill of his wide shoulders, the trim waist and the lean line of his buttocks in the expensively tailored trousers.

'Then becoming my lover has no appeal for you either, hmm?' He swung round, eyeing her morosely. 'I'd be a very generous lover while our liaison lasted.'

Generous with everything but his love. That was pledged to Frederica, the unacknowledged mother of his child. She shook her head dismissively.

'Generosity is more than paying the bills, Alexos. It's generosity of spirit that makes a marriage work...the willingness to give and take, the genuine desire to be faithful and honest to one's partner despite past loyalties...' She choked into silence as incipient tears gathered behind her eyes.

'And you're saying I'm not capable of those things?' Anger thickened his voice.

'Oh, I'm sure you are!' She took refuge in scorn to hide her pain. 'Towards the woman you still love, but not towards me!'

'The woman I still love?' His dark brows drew together. 'What nonsense is this? It's not I who still mourns a broken engagement!'

It was all too much. Since the previous evening she'd been near to breaking-point, the heavy weight of what she'd discovered growing more and more intolerable to bear in silence. If Alexos had had the dignity to remain silent and accept her decision she might have succeeded in leaving without telling him what she knew, but now, as she was confronted with his barefaced lies, the dam of her misery broke.

'Don't lie to me, Alexos!' Her voice, pitched low, quivered with emotion. 'I know the truth about you and Frederica!'

At least he made no attempt to deny it. In fact, his very stillness in the face of her accusation indicted him. She had expected either an attempt at bluff or an angry explosion of guilt; instead there was a short silence, broken only by her own uneven breathing before Alexos said quietly, 'Exactly what do you know about Frederica and me?'

The emptiness in her was complete, and she'd gone so far that there was no point in stopping now.

'You're in love with your brother's wife and she feels the same way about you,' she said tonelessly. 'Don't try to deny it, Alexos—I saw the way she's been looking at you ever since we've been here. I know it was her on the phone pretending to be the manageress of the Hotel Belvedere. And then...then...I overheard what she said to you last night in the garden: you cooked up the whole thing between you, because you didn't want your brother to know how you both still felt...' Her voice tailed off as her throat became too dry to allow her to continue speaking.

Alexos said something that could only have been profane, staring at her as if she'd gone mad, his face drained of colour, his eyes black and empty as if he'd been punched in the solar plexus and emptied of air.

'You don't understand, Ilona...' He started to speak, then stopped, as if aware that anything he could say would only condemn him. Into the aching silence that followed there came a sharp rat-a-tat on the bedroom door. It was Alexos who strode across, pulling it open, his face still a set mask of shock as his half-brother was revealed on the threshold.

'Later, Nikos!' he growled, preparing to shut the door in the younger man's face.

'Now, Alexos!' Nikos's voice was surprisingly firm, devoid of the slight deference it had always before assumed in Alexos's presence. 'I want to talk to both you and Ilona, together.'

'Damn it, can't you see when you're not wanted?' Alexos snarled, preparing to close the door in his face, only to be prevented as Nikos insisted,

'Let me in. What I've got to say will only take a few minutes. But it must be said.'

'Let him in, Alexos,' Ilona added her voice to Nikos's pleading. 'There's nothing he can say I don't already know.'

For a moment she thought Alexos would ignore her plea, then wordlessly he inclined his head, retreating a stride to allow his half-brother to enter.

The younger man hesitated for a brief moment then seemed to gather his strength together.

'Frederica and I have been having a long talk, Alexos, and we've come to the conclusion that, since Ilona is going to be your wife, she should know the truth about you—the whole truth; the only truth.'

'No!' Alexos's voice was hoarse. 'Nikos, I forbid it! There was an agreement.'

Nikos made a sharp gesture with his head. 'Yes, but you've been outvoted—two to one.'

'You don't know what you're doing!' Anguish tortured the hard-sculptured lines of Alexos's face as Ilona's heart ached with compassion for him. 'Ilona and I——'

'You're wrong.' Nikos's young face looked strained, but his voice remained steady. 'For the first time in many years I'm doing what's right.' His gaze left his half-brother's agonised countenance to meet Ilona's clear-eyed appraisal. 'The facts are these, Ilona: Alexos served three years in gaol for the unlawful killing of a man, but he wasn't guilty. I was the one who committed the crime. I was the one who should have paid the penalty.'

CHAPTER ELEVEN

ILONA'S world shattered like a broken kaleidoscope, the pieces disintegrating, failing to reform into a discernible pattern. She could only stand motionless, staring at the two men, feeling the tension thrumming between them like a high-powered cable.

It was Nikos who broke the unbearable silence, addressing her directly.

'Frederica and Alexos were betrothed as children, you see, but because my brother spent most of his time away from Kaphos they hardly knew each other. I, on the other hand, spent most of my life here. Frederica and I were friends as children, and as we grew older that friendship matured, became serious.' A tinge of colour flared across his tanned cheekbones.

'We became lovers. Oh, we both felt guilty about forming a relationship behind Alexos's back, but what we felt for each other was too strong to ignore; besides, we knew he cared nothing for her. The whole principle of betrothal was outdated and absurd.' He paused briefly, then continued steadily. 'Then Frederica became pregnant and we knew it was imperative we told Alexos. We needed his help and understanding because it was a desperate situation for Frederica. I wanted to marry her, but because of the understanding between our two families I had to enlist my brother's help.'

'You've said enough, Nikos!' Alexos's harsh voice broke into his monologue. 'Ilona isn't interested in your lurid past.'

'Then she should be, because it's irrevocably en-twined with yours!'

'Not any more!' It was as if he'd been injected with a sudden surge of energy. 'Get out of here, Nikos, before I throw you out. You've already said enough—more than enough.'

The younger man hesitated, his resolve threatened by the sheer power of Alexos's antagonism, allowing his eyes to linger on Ilona's shocked face before returning to regard his brother. 'Perhaps you're right,' he conceded slowly. 'But at least she knows the truth now. I'll leave it to you to tell her exactly what happened.'

Then, seeming to draw on an inner courage, he turned to face Ilona, saying firmly, 'Make him tell you every-thing that happened, Ilona, because, if he doesn't, Frederica and I will.' Then, turning towards Alexos, he added quietly, 'It was always a secret you had no right to keep from any woman you asked to be your wife.'

Three strides took him to the door and beyond it.

'Ignore him.' Alexos said gruffly as soon as the catch closed. 'Go back to Crete and forget everything you've heard. Nothing Nikos has said alters the fact that you can't, by your own admission, face life with a man who has a criminal record.'

'But Xeni is Nikos's daughter!' Ilona cried out passionately, her carefully worked-out scenario in smithereens at her feet.

'Of course. Everyone knows that.' Alexos stared at her as if she were mad.

'I—I thought she was yours,' she admitted painfully. The whole edifice of evidence she'd built up against him was crumbling and she was in danger of becoming buried in the debris.

'Mine!' Indigo eyes regarded her with astonishment beneath knitted brows.

Her mouth trembling, she fought to put her suspicions into a logical progression of words. 'I—I worked out that she'd been born six months after Nikos and Frederica were married, you see, and I thought he'd married her in your stead to avoid a scandal, because you were... you were...'

'Detained elsewhere?' he supplied drily. 'Dear God...' He vented a harsh laugh. 'Is *that* why you had a change of heart about becoming my wife? Because you believed I was in love with Frederica?'

She nodded, feeling an aching void where her heart should have been. 'I thought you'd only brought me here so that Nikos would be fooled into believing your affair was over,' she confessed as Alexos stood motionless, his expression unreadable.

As fierce pangs of regret brought stinging tears to her eyes she turned away. There was still so much she didn't understand, but, beside the enormity of the mistake she'd made, even Nikos's shattering revelation of Alexos's innocence took second place.

'Ilona—wait!' Moving swiftly, Alexos seized her, pulling her round to face him. 'That was it? All of it?' Before her eyes his face seemed to mutate, lose its granite-hardness, as his voice became husky with emotion. 'That was the only reason you decided to go back to Crete? You were jealous of Frederica? You believed I'd always loved her and we were planning to use your presence to deceive my brother?'

'Yes.' The admission was torn from bone-dry lips. There was no way now she could save even a fragment of her pride. No way she wanted to. 'It wasn't just the atmosphere when you met again or the way Frederica looked at you with such love in her eyes, such devotion...' Her voice faltered momentarily, but somehow she must make him understand why she'd jumped to conclusions.

She couldn't expect his forgiveness, but she could hope for his understanding. Her voice dropped to a whisper. 'You see, I couldn't help overhearing what she said to you in the garden last night about having been betrothed to you and the moments of joy and love you'd given her.' She paused to swallow, to get her voice under control. 'It all seemed to fit.'

Despite all her efforts, tears stung her eyes. 'I knew you didn't love me, but until then I thought perhaps we could still build a future together, find a kind of contentment together...' Miserably she dipped her head, unable to continue as emotion temporarily froze the muscles of her throat.

'So when you said you couldn't share your life with a criminal——?'

'It was an excuse to save my own face,' she admitted sombrely. 'I felt stupid and humiliated that I'd allowed myself to be lured into a trap in which so many people risked being hurt.'

'Listen to me, Ilona,' his voice was strangely hoarse as he lifted her chin with his powerful hand, forcing her to meet his steady gaze, 'you know *now* that I'm not in love with Frederica—or she with me, that we've never cared for each other that way; but nothing else has altered. You must ignore everything Nikos has claimed because the fact is I still have a prison record and nothing is going to wipe that out. I was tried, found guilty and sentenced. That is the truth and nothing, *nothing*, is going to change it.'

'But Nikos wasn't lying, was he?' Her feelings rose in a furious spiral of anger and incomprehension as she thought of the suffering Alexos had undergone on his half-brother's behalf. 'Why, Alexos? Oh, why did you take the blame for something that wasn't your fault?'

For a few seconds he scrutinised her white face and she thought he would deny her the satisfaction of the truth; that by doubting his integrity she'd forfeited every right to learn about his past. Then he sighed.

'I was on the mainland when Nikos phoned me and told me about Frederica's pregnancy,' he began with no apparent emotion on his dark features. 'Of course, I returned to Kaphos immediately. I admit I was furious, not because he'd taken over my territory but because Frederica's father was a tough Greek of the old school, and my brother should have exercised self-control before exposing her to the kind of ordeal she was likely to undergo at her father's hands.'

His strong jawline clenched. 'Dealing with such a man was way outside Nikos's experience—and he knew it!'

'Go on,' Ilona begged softly into the silence.

He made a gesture of despair with both hand. 'Nikos was also fearful of facing Theo, knowing he still harboured hopes of Frederica and myself becoming married. He and her father were old friends, comrades in the Resistance, and such bonds are not easily denied or insulted. So at Nikos's request instead of going to Belvedere I arranged to meet both him and Frederica in one of the harbour tavernas to decide the best plan of action.'

Once more he paused, the anguish of recall plainly discernible on his harshly drawn features as he turned away from her, thrusting his hands into the pockets of his trousers and taking a few strides before turning once more to meet her compassionate gaze.

'My brother suddenly seemed to grow in stature after one or two drinks and said he'd take Frederica back to her own house and confront her father with what had happened between them, stating his intention of marrying her with or without his permission.' He shrugged his powerful shoulders. 'I vetoed that idea. Frederica's father was hot-tempered and not beyond thrashing my brother unmercifully. Not that he didn't deserve it, but there were more important issues to be considered. I told Nikos *I* would take Frederica back and explain to her father. Apart from the fact I wasn't personally responsible for her condition, I felt better able to protect her from her father's fury.'

He paused, the turmoil mirrored on his face a proof that he was reliving the night that had changed his life, resuming with a conscious effort.

'While we'd had our heads together a party of tourists had come into the taverna, a group of young men much the worse for alcohol and bent on making nuisances of themselves. One was particularly insulting to Frederica, and when I pointed this out to him there was a bit of a scrap and I sent him sprawling. That's where it should have ended.'

'Instead?' she prompted softly as he lapsed into silence.

'When Frederica and I left for her home two of them followed us. Our path led through the pine-woods and it was there they attacked us. One went for me, and while I was defending myself the other one, the one I'd previously punched, grabbed hold of Frederica.' He smiled grimly, his eyes devoid of humour. 'I soon settled the one who'd gone for me, and in a matter of seconds I'd hauled the other one away from Frederica. He was hopelessly drunk and I hit him hard enough to bruise him, to punish him for daring to touch her. He just reeled away.'

'But Nikos said...' Ilona's large brown eyes scanned his solemn face, still not understanding, 'Nikos said that it was *he* who——'

'Was responsible for his death.' He sighed. 'Yes, I know. Nikos had been following us, you see. He was full of anger and frustration, furious that I'd prevented him from confessing everything to Frederica's father.'

'But he'd asked for your help!'

'Help, yes,' he agreed tonelessly. 'But by taking away from him the dignity of shouldering his own responsibility with his future father-in-law I'd humiliated him. It was his role to protect Frederica—not mine—and he'd made up his mind to do just that. So you see, in a way, I was just as responsible for what happened as Nikos was.' He expelled his breath in a long sigh. 'I turned to comfort Frederica at the moment my brother came storming out of the shadows, intent on revenge. He was so enraged that he didn't realise how drunk the other man was, or how dazed...until...he'd landed half a dozen undefended blows to his head and face.'

'Oh, dear God!' The exclamation was forced from her lips as Alexos began to pace up and down the room, shoulders hunched, hand still thrust deep into his trouser pockets.

'The man just folded up and lay there motionless, and Nikos seemed stunned, unaware of how serious the situation was. Frederica was crying from shock, so I made Nikos take her back to her father, swore them both to remain silent, while I went for help. But I already knew it was too late to save him.'

'And they let you take the blame!' Horrified, she could hardly force the words out. 'Why, oh, why did you do it? You must have been mad to sacrifice your whole future for—for...' she stormed passionately, tears beginning to run down her cheeks as words failed her.

'My younger brother's happiness with the woman he loved and who was carrying his child?'

Suddenly he was at her side and she was being held tightly, her outrage being controlled with gentle purpose, Alexos's hand stroking and caressing her to peace, his cheek nuzzling hers, his voice crooning intimate words of love and understanding over and over again until her body shuddered to a trembling halt.

'You have to understand the situation, *agape mou*,' he murmured. 'A man had been killed in a fight. There was always going to be a high price to pay for that. Fortunately his companion had seen only me before he ran away. If I'd told the police exactly what happened it would have been Nikos in the dock instead of me—and think how greater a tragedy that would have been.'

'It would have been justice,' Ilona whispered and felt his lips caress her forehead.

'Who for, hmm? It was imperative Frederica marry my brother as soon as possible for the child's sake. My parents were going to suffer terribly anyway, but to Calliope I was only a stepson and my father and I have lived apart most of our lives. Then there was Nikos himself—not twenty-two years of age. A man in many things, yes, but not in the ways of the world. He'd lived all his life on Kaphos, cushioned against harsh reality. He was young and good to look at...' Alexos's voice deepened, became almost strident. 'He would never have survived the vice and moral perversion he would have found in gaol.'

'And you? What about you, Alexos *mou*?' Ilona's voice was raw with anguish. 'You weren't much older, and you...' She raised her hand to trace loving fingers over the hard, fine bones of his face, the tender curves of his mouth '...you are very, *very* good to look at.'

He seized her trembling hand, kissing its fingers before entwining them with his own. 'But I was tough. My father had seen to that. He'd made me so that I had no fear of any man. It was a precious gift and I owed it to him to use it.' He sighed as Ilona laid her fair head against his chest and he saw the trail of moisture on her cheek.

'Ilona, my love, don't keep crying,' he said tenderly. 'I wasn't without blame. I was betrothed to Frederica and cared nothing for it. I was insensitive enough to believe I could enjoy myself in Athens, taking my pleasure where it was so freely offered, while all the time she would be waiting, eager and innocent, prepared to be my wife and bear my children if and when the fancy to settle down took me. When Nikos confessed their feelings for each other I saw for the first time how truly selfish my own life had been. Hell! I'd had no consideration for anyone. Calliope, who had loved me like her own flesh and blood; Theo, who had wanted a man for a son and had begotten a strutting cockerel, all voice and no heart; the women who provided an occasional night's pleasure and whose names were forgotten by morning...' He laughed bitterly. 'Even the original quarrel at the taverna might have been prevented if I'd used my head instead of my fists.'

'Whatever you were, whatever you'd done, you hadn't been the cause of a man's death. Nikos should never have let you take the blame,' she insisted angrily.

'Hush, *mahtia mou*.' He spoke the soft endearment as if he truly loved her, smoothing her silky hair with gentle fingers. 'I gave him no choice. I took the decision and he obeyed me as he'd done when we were children together. By the time the case was heard he had taken Frederica to Athens and they were man and wife. Shortly afterwards she became very ill with toxaemia and nearly lost Xeni. For weeks she was kept in a darkened room while Nikos haunted the hospital. He had more than enough to worry about without trying to get me to change my mind.'

Ilona's mouth tightened mutinously. 'I don't care what you say, I can't feel any sympathy for him.'

'Then perhaps you should,' he told her gently. 'My punishment is over, but Nikos's never will be until the day he dies. He carries a terrible burden on his young shoulders, the burden of silence and guilt. If you think he isn't suffering for what he did—and the consequences—then you're wrong. And what he did a few minutes ago took great courage.'

'But your father—oh, Alexos! Theo should know what you did and why!'

'No.' Alexos smiled down at her indignant face. 'It's taken a long time and there've been faults on both sides, but my father and I are beginning to come to terms with our differences. Nothing good would come of raking over old coals, only more pain and distress for everyone concerned.'

'But——'

'But nothing.' There was a glowing warmth in the dark eyes that met her tremulous regard. 'If you really care so much about me then the remedy is in your own hands. Give me the chance to fulfil myself as a husband and father.'

'Are you sure you still want me?' she asked almost inaudibly. 'After all the dreadful things I said to you— after what I believed?'

'I'm a humane judge,' he said softly. 'I'm prepared to accept your plea of self-defence—provided you swear that you no longer believe that Frederica and I are carrying a burning torch for each other.'

'I swear it.' She gave him a tentative smile. 'Although I stand by my first impression—she does love you very much, Alexos.'

'She loves me like a brother-in-law,' he agreed smoothly. 'That's all.'

'She loves you like the man who gave her so many moments of joy and love—with her husband.'

'Precisely—as long as you understand that, I see no reason why you and Frederica shouldn't become the best of friends. Believe me, she couldn't have been more delighted when I phoned her in Athens that afternoon and told her I'd met the girl I wanted to marry but that I needed her help to ensure she didn't escape me. She agreed immediately to lie on my behalf.'

'You told her that?' Ilona asked wonderingly. 'But you didn't even appear to like me!'

'I liked you too much—that was the problem,' he admitted with a wry twist of his mouth. 'But I was still adjusting to being a free man and I was afraid to trust my instincts. Besides, you were mourning for your own broken relationship, and the last thing I wanted was for you to turn to me on the rebound, so I found myself fighting my own feelings for both our sakes. I thought that if I offered you material wealth and well-being it would be a foundation on which we could build our personal relationship over a period of time.

'Damn it, Ilona!' His voice harshened. 'With a background like mine, what else have I to offer a woman? When I took the blame for what occurred in the pinewoods I'd no thought of marriage on my mind. It was only when I met you and realised how much I wanted you as my wife that I realised how high the odds were stacked against me.'

'You—are you saying that you love me?' she asked hesitantly, her heart pounding like the thunder of a race-horse's hoofs on sun-baked turf.

'From the first moment I saw you,' he confirmed art-lessly. 'Are you trying to tell me that you didn't know. I thought women always knew these things.'

'Not me.' She shook her head, bewildered.

'Well, believe it, then,' he assured her huskily. 'That's why I was so angry when I went back to the El Greco the next morning and was told you intended to return to England; why I was determined to do anything within my power to keep you with me. Even then I knew you were the woman I wanted to marry.'

Her whole body glowing with his reassurance, Ilona smiled up into his sombre eyes. 'But how could you possibly have been so sure, Alexos? I mean, all those other women you mentioned—had you never wanted to marry one of them and then decided against it later?'

'Never!' he said fervently. 'And there weren't that many. Sex without love is an empty pleasure—it satisfies the body but leaves the soul starving. It was a lesson I learned very quickly. It's one that Frederica knows full well, which is why she lied for me: why she persuaded Nikos they had to break their vow of silence.'

Ilona's heart leapt in her throat as he stared down at her. The beautiful indigo eyes were pregnable, unde-fended by pride or caution, as he said softly, '*S'agapo, kardia mou*—I love you, Ilona. I've waited a long time to be able to say that to any woman, and it's not just because you're beautiful and desirable, or because you awaken all my protective instincts, or because you speak

my language or because you've won over my father's
heart. It's because I can't help myself. When I'm in your
company I feel whole, complete. I never want to lose
that feeling—never.'

'Alexos...' She breathed his name, letting his words
run like honey over her self-inflicted wounds, healing
them.

He searched her face with tortured eyes then caught
her to him, holding her close, his voice broken and rough.
'Just give me the chance to prove to you that I'm not
the arrogant, unfeeling, conniving brute I must have
seemed...'

'Oh, Alexos,' she sighed. 'Surely you know...?'

'Wait!' For a few seconds she stood alone as he took
a stride towards the bedside table; then he was back in
front of her, a deep pink rose held between his fingers.
'You once told me that if you loved me I could be a
pauper and still buy you with a single rose...' He extended his arm, offering her the bloom.

Too full of emotion to speak, Ilona nodded, accepting the flower, only to let it fall gently to the floor
as she found herself enfolded to the muscular strength
of Alexos's vibrant body, waves of heady desire storming
through every cell of her being.

This time there was no holding back as Alexos's
shaking masculine fingers slid her simple clothes from
her body, his expressive eyes worshipping her as much
as his tender touch, before he lifted her on to the bed.

Lying there, her head propped up on one arm,
watching unashamedly as he struggled out of his own
clothes, she was bewitched by the scent of his sun-warm
skin, the smooth power of his muscled arms, the cor-
rugated leanness of his flat abdomen, the sheer overpowering beauty of his potent masculinity.

Tentatively she stroked his body as he joined her, running her fingers over his chest, following the rib-cage, sliding her exploratory hand across the heated flesh of his abdomen.

When he lowered his body to touch her own she gasped, startled by the power and speed of her own arousal as his hands touched her breasts and his mouth worshipped the burgeoning apices.

'Please...' She forced the word from pleasure-swollen lips. 'Please...' Her hands reached out, begging for the solace of his body, craving it.

'*Kardia mou, mahtia mou*...my heart, my eyes,' he breathed, and gave himself to her keeping.

She accepted him easily and painlessly, crying out loud with the simplicity and perfection of their consummation, levering her hips up, grasping the smooth hollows of his loins and pushing her own body deep against his, scarcely aware of what she was doing to him as her body made its own claims against his invasion.

Alexos had never made love to a virgin. The few women in his life had been transient and unimportant, satisfying only because he'd allowed them to arouse the need they then satisfied. They hadn't cared for him, enjoying only his potency and performance. It had been a game and one that had grown to sicken him long before his enforced celibacy.

With Ilona it was different. He loved her and he wanted to make love to her with all the time and finesse and control he knew he was capable of. But it wasn't like that. It was indescribable. The barrier of her purity parted with an awe-inspiring ease and, far from rejecting him in pain or fear, as he'd half expected, her body welcomed him with a response that he realised with an incredulous horror was going to lead to disaster.

'I'm sorry, my darling.' His breathing had steadied after the violent culmination of fulfilment. 'Next time I'll make it better for you, I promise.'

'Different perhaps—not better.' She smiled up at him, her heart in her eyes. 'Nothing is ever better than the first. The first step, the first exam passed——'

'The first union between lovers,' he finished for her softly. 'Let's pray your father phones us without delay with his blessing. When I came to your room I wasn't prepared for a happy ending, and no one is going to doubt that I am the legitimate father of the future heir to Belvedere!'

'He'll approve—I know he will.' She ran one soft hand down Alexos's suntanned thigh. 'Oh, and we'll have to get in touch with Aristide and with the El Greco...' She paused, frowning. 'Whatever did you say to the manager to make him change his mind about me?'

Laughter glowed in the depth of Alexos's eyes. 'Oh, I just told him that you were a model of virtue and propriety...and that I was a major shareholder in the company that owned the actual bricks and mortar of the El Greco, where he had been granted a franchise to operate hotel services.'

'Faradaxis Construction owns the El Greco?' She stared at him in astonishment. 'But you only had to tell Manolis that and there's no way you would have been refused a drink!'

'Precisely.' He smiled at her indignant expression. 'And that, *agape mou*, was exactly what I was going to do when you intervened.'

'Then what I did was all for nothing!'

'How can you say that,' he asked softly, 'when your reckless action determined my future—*our* future? I've already told you it was at that moment of your intervention that I fell utterly and completely in love with you. Surely keeping silent isn't such an unforgivable crime in the circumstances?'

'I'll have to give it some thought.' She pretended uncertainty. 'I'll let you know my decision when I've cancelled the room you've booked for me.'

She made to move off the bed, only to be held in place by one strong, muscular arm, which latched around her waist.

'Where's your sense of priorities, *yineka*?' Alexos growled. 'As far as my future wife is concerned, my needs take precedence over everyone and everything else!'

A long time later, as they lay once more in the totally consuming embrace of lovers at peace with themselves and the world, Ilona knew with a deep satisfaction that there was nothing she could not forgive him and that both she and Alexos had truly 'come home'—and that this time it would be forever.

THE PERFECT GIFT FOR MOTHER'S DAY

Specially selected for you – four tender and heartwarming Romances written by popular authors.

LEGEND OF LOVE -
Melinda Cross

AN IMPERFECT AFFAIR -
Natalie Fox

LOVE IS THE KEY -
Mary Lyons

LOVE LIKE GOLD -
Valerie Parv

Available from February 1993   Price: £6.80

Accept 4 FREE Romances and 2 FREE gifts

Mills & Boon

FROM READER SERVICE

An irresistible invitation from Mills & Boon Reader Service. Please accept our offer of 4 free Romances, a CUDDLY TEDDY and a special MYSTERY GIFT... Then, if you choose, go on to enjoy 6 captivating Romances every month for just £1.70 each, postage and packing free. Plus our FREE Newsletter with author news, competitions and much more.

Send the coupon below to:
Reader Service, FREEPOST,
PO Box 236, Croydon,
Surrey CR9 9EL.

NO STAMP REQUIRED

Yes! Please rush me 4 Free Romances and 2 free gifts!
Please also reserve me a Reader Service Subscription. If I decide to subscribe I can look forward to receiving 6 brand new Romances each month for just £10.20, post and packing free.
If I choose not to subscribe I shall write to you within 10 days - I can keep the books and gifts whatever I decide. I may cancel or suspend my subscription at any time. I am over 18 years of age.

Ms/Mrs/Miss/Mr ———————————————— EP30R

Address —————————————————————

———————————————————————————

Postcode ——————— Signature ———————

Next Month's Romances

Each month you can choose from a wide variety of romance with Mills & Boon. Below are the new titles to look out for next month, why not ask either Mills & Boon Reader Service or your Newsagent to reserve you a copy of the titles you want to buy — just tick the titles you would like and either post to Reader Service or take it to any Newsagent and ask them to order your books.

Please save me the following titles:		Please tick √
AN OUTRAGEOUS PROPOSAL	Miranda Lee	
RICH AS SIN	Anne Mather	
ELUSIVE OBSESSION	Carole Mortimer	
AN OLD-FASHIONED GIRL	Betty Neels	
DIAMOND HEART	Susanne McCarthy	
DANCE WITH ME	Sophie Weston	
BY LOVE ALONE	Kathryn Ross	
ELEGANT BARBARIAN	Catherine Spencer	
FOOTPRINTS IN THE SAND	Anne Weale	
FAR HORIZONS	Yvonne Whittal	
HOSTILE INHERITANCE	Rosalie Ash	
THE WATERS OF EDEN	Joanna Neil	
FATEFUL DESIRE	Carol Gregor	
HIS COUSIN'S KEEPER	Miriam Macgregor	
SOMETHING WORTH FIGHTING FOR	Kristy McCallum	
LOVE'S UNEXPECTED TURN	Barbara McMahon	

If you would like to order these books in addition to your regular subscription from Mills & Boon Reader Service please send £1.70 per title to: Mills & Boon Reader Service, P.O. Box 236, Croydon, Surrey, CR9 3RU, quote your Subscriber No:...
(If applicable) and complete the name and address details below. Alternatively, these books are available from many local Newsagents including W.H.Smith, J.Menzies, Martins and other paperback stockists from 12th February 1993.

Name:..

Address:..

....Post Code:.........................

To Retailer: If you would like to stock M&B books please contact your regular book/magazine wholesaler for details.

You may be mailed with offers from other reputable companies as a result of this application.
If you would rather not take advantage of these opportunities please tick box ☐